A CANDLELIGHT ROMANCE

CANDLELIGHT ROMANCES

231 HOLD ME FOREVER, Melissa Blakely
234 ONE LOVE FOREVER, Meredith Babeaux Brucker
235 FORBIDDEN YEARNINGS, Candice Arkham
236 PRECIOUS MOMENTS, Suzanne Roberts
237 SURRENDER TO LOVE, Helen Nuelle
238 THE HEART HAS REASONS, Stephanie Kincaid
241 THE HEART'S HORIZONS, Anne Shore
242 A LIFETIME TO LOVE, Ann Dabney
243 WHISPERS OF THE HEART, Anne Shore
244 LOVE'S OWN DREAM, Jacqueline Hacsi
249 THE SEARCHING HEART, Suzanne Roberts
252 A TROPICAL AFFAIR, Elizabeth Beresford
254 VICTIM OF LOVE, Lee Canaday
256 WINTER KISSES, SUMMER LOVE, Anne Shore
258 HIGHLAND LOVESONG, Stephanie Kincaid
259 ECHOES OF LOVE, Elizabeth Beresford
260 SPLENDORS OF THE HEART, Candice Arkham
261 PROMISE BY MOONLIGHT, Anne Shore
262 ALOHA, LOVE, Bella Jarrett
264 CLOSE TO THE STARS, Meredith Babeaux Brucker
502 THE LEGEND OF LOVE, Louise Bergstrom
503 SUMMER MAGIC, Frances Carfi Matranga
507 THE WINDS OF LOVE, Virginia Myers
509 LOVE'S PROMISE, Nina Pykare
511 WINTER'S LOVING TOUCH, Jacqueline Hacsi
513 PROMISE IN PARADISE, Lorena McCourtney
516 RENDEZVOUS IN ATHENS, Jessica Eliot
517 THE GOLDEN PIRATE, Phyllis Pianka
519 SEARCH FOR YESTERDAY, Barbara Doyle
522 STOLEN DREAMS, Stephanie Kincaid
525 LOVE'S SWEET ILLUSION, Suzanne Roberts
526 DESTINY IN ROME, Frances Carfi Matranga
531 FIRST A DREAM, Marie Pershing
532 PASSIONATE SUMMER, Belle Thorne
535 LOVE IS LIKE THAT, Irene Lawrence
536 EMBERS OF THE HEART, Candice Arkham
540 THE LONG ENCHANTMENT, Helen Nuelle
541 SECRET LONGINGS, Nancy Kennedy
546 LEGACY OF THE HEART, Lorena McCourtney
547 FAREWELL TO ALEXANDRIA, Suzanne Roberts
552 OMEN FOR LOVE, Esther Boyd
553 MAYBE TOMORROW, Marie Pershing

THE
MIDNIGHT
EMBRACE

Barbara Doyle

A CANDLELIGHT ROMANCE

Published by
Dell Publishing Co., Inc.
1 Dag Hammarskjold Plaza
New York, New York 10017

Copyright © 1980 by Barbara Doyle

All rights reserved. No part of this book may be reproduced or transmitted in any form or by any means, electronic or mechanical, including photocopying, recording or by any information storage and retrieval system, without the written permission of the Publisher, except where permitted by law.

Dell ® TM 681510, Dell Publishing Co., Inc.

ISBN: 0-440-15132-5

Printed in the United States of America
First printing—April 1980

Chapter 1

Aunt Agatha had always been one for good common sense and practicality. In fact, many were the times that neighbors and friends had to cajole her into doing something in a more frivolous vein than her daily share of mundane but responsible chores. "The good Lord put a brain in my head and He didn't put it there to waste it on nonsense," she was heard to say on a number of occasions. And yet when she could be coerced into attending an outing or participating in a random bridge game, her eyes twinkled merrily as if she were waiting a long while just to be allowed to join one of these events. But still, no one ever intimated that Aunt Agatha was square. To the contrary, she often delighted in listening to others' accounts of varied social escapades or flighty shopping sprees and never clucked against any of these things, as long as she was not part of them.

It seemed that ever since Terrace was a child, Aunt Agatha had walked around with the look of a person who had the weight of the world on her shoulders. And this visage never seemed to leave her or most often not, whether she bustled around her own two-story wood-frame house—and this is what she did most as she was a very meticulous lady—or made a short trip to the small shopping area nearby, or even when kneeling in church on Sunday mornings—the look was always prominent.

One could even take into account the very few times that Agatha Warren did nothing, and this was indeed a rarity. When this took place, it was always in the vicinity of the porch that framed three quarters of her old Victorian house. And if Aunt Agatha did idle some time away there, it was sure to be on the old wicker rocking chair with its two foam rubber avocado-green pillows that matched the avocado shutters of the house. There Aunt Agatha could be seen rocking furiously and using the time, in her practical way, to solve some small household problem.

It was this constant preoccupation and dedication to the practical side of life by Aunt Agatha which left Terrace incredulous of the fact that she was now high above the Atlantic on her way to a carefree holiday in Ireland.

Terrace could remember very clearly Aunt Agatha's face that graduation morning as she presented her with the certificate that stated she had completed her studies at the San Francisco School of Interior Design. The woman's expression had gone blank for a moment and then her lips parted into the sweetest of smiles, while her shoulders relaxed and she let out a very deep sigh. It was then that she confessed to Terrace that for many years she had saved her pennies in an old coffee can for such an auspicious occasion. And with that she had produced from her purse the long white envelope that contained the round-trip ticket to Dublin.

The surprise was so contrary to all of Agatha's practical upbringing that Terrace protested vehemently at first to the capricious undertaking. Yet, as she looked into her aunt's eyes, she knew that the trip would please her greatly.

"You deserve it, Terrace," she had said. "You've been a good niece. I didn't know what to expect when you were left in my care after your parents died in that accident. But we did a good job, you and I. You gave me a lot of pleasure and now I'd like you to have some fun."

So she had left San Francisco with Aunt Agatha waving at her from the observation deck as the big jet took off for New York. And after a day's layover that allowed her to visit the Empire State Building, Statue of Liberty, and Hudson River, she boarded the plane she was now on that would land in Ireland.

Somewhere in her memory she recalled her fourth-grade geography teacher mentioning the fact that New York was on the same parallel as Madrid. The trip to Ireland, then, was on a far more northern route than her point of embarkation. At first she had thought that this was the reason why her body felt chilled the last hour of the flight. Then she realized that the feeling was due to the excitement welling up within her over the realization that the trip was not a dream but indeed an actuality. She could not deny the fact that she had some trepidations about going off to a strange country by herself. Yet, Aunt Ag had raised her to be self-reliant and the misapprehensions did not last long, nor did they deter her from making the trip at all. The plane had been sparsely filled with passengers and she was thankful of this. She did not feel in the right frame of mind to make small talk with her fellow passengers, as her thoughts were filled with

7

scenes of what her next few weeks would be like. She had even accepted a pile of diversified magazines from the stewardess, and although she heaped them impressively on her lap with the top one opened to a middle page, she hardly read more than two lines throughout the journey.

Again her mind leaped to Aunt Agatha and the small sacrifices that she had to make over the years to save up for the trip. She was grateful then that her aunt had suggested contacting her father's family in Dublin where she could stay for the first week or so until she became oriented to her surroundings. She remembered hearing Aunt Agatha mention her Dublin relatives a few times during her childhood. Yet the stories were few and quite vague as Agatha was her mother's sister and not very familiar with that side of the family. Agatha did mention, however, that it would be interesting for her to finally meet these relations.

Her thoughts were suddenly interrupted by the stewardess who was making a pilgrimage down the aisle collecting pillows that were previously distributed after takeoff from Kennedy airport. She felt that this was a sign that they were nearing their destination and again she sensed a ripple of excitement within her. Aunt Agatha, she said to herself, what have you done to me. I should be nicely content in my usual schedule of boredom instead of preparing to embark at some strange international city. Then she reprimanded herself. Of course she was excited about the trip and she would not allow any more misapprehensions to enter her mind.

She folded her hands on her lap in a gesture of definite decision and began to look out the window to

8

concentrate on the clouds before her optimistic determination would waver.

Night had changed into early dawn halfway across the Atlantic to accommodate the time difference between continents. Although she felt like curling into a self-protective heap in her seat for a short nap, she knew that she should keep awake, as it would soon be time to freshen her makeup and comb her hair before touchdown at Dublin. She wondered which member of her father's family would be at the Arrivals gate to meet her. The note that arrived from Dublin in answer to her own was short, but it did say she would be met.

The white and purple puffs of cloud that had accompanied them on most of the flight were just beginning to part, and she caught her first glimpse of the Emerald Isle. Green of every shade made up a potpourri of landscape as the plane lost altitude and the various landing instruction lights were flicked on for the passengers.

She was able to leave her seat to freshen her makeup and make it back just as the stewardess announced that seat belts should be fastened.

Although the landing had been smooth, she had closed her eyes tightly until they had touched on land and the jet motors were turned off. That was smooth, she thought, and at the same time she said a quick prayer that the rest of the trip would be as pleasant as her landing.

There was no difficulty picking out the person who was to meet her after clearing customs. He was hanging over the low barrier, his hair as auburn as hers was, and his face almost a mirrored replica of her own.

9

She could not help but slow her steps as she noticed him—as the longing from her childhood for a brother came into her mind. The same reaction seemed to come over him, as his eyes widened and then a smile crossed his face as he extended his hand.

"Cead mile failte," he said as he half embraced her and then took her one suitcase. "There'd be no mistakin' lass which family you're here to visit," he continued in an obvious put-on of the Irish dialect. "I'm Padrig, a first cousin of yours and I'm here to give you welcome on behalf of the rest of the family." The lilt was gone now, and although there was a twang of accent to his words, it was close to, yet a little short of, the English accents she had heard.

"I'm Terrace Connors."

"Yes indeed," he said, smiling. "Was your flight pleasant?" he inquired as he led her to the parking area to the right of the terminal.

"Yes, it was quite a smooth flight," she answered, remembering her apprehensions.

"I'm sure glad of that, sure-an'-I wished you luck on your journey here," he said, falling back into a heavy brogue. And then he laughed, "I'm trying to make you feel at ease with the type of speech that you were possibly expecting. But truthfully, the brogue you hear exemplified on Irish day in the States is from the region of Kerry. The Dublin speech is a little quieter and more reserved," he said as he indicated a maroon Mercedes and helped her in after he had placed her luggage on the back seat.

"I guess I hadn't thought much about it," she said to him as he entered the driver's seat and started the

10

car. "To tell you the truth, I could not imagine what to expect here—everything happened so quickly."

"The trip was a surprise then?" he asked, throwing her a quick look. "You're an artist, Terrace?"

"Well, not exactly. I'm an interior decorator, or, I hope to be. I just graduated from school and was about to look for a position when Aunt Agatha suggested I take a holiday."

"Interior decorating should be an interesting line to follow. With all the new housing being erected all around the outskirts of Dublin, you will probably make a killing here."

Her head snapped quickly in his direction. "I don't intend to stay in Ireland," she said slowly and distinctly. "After a few weeks I'll have to return to the States."

"I see," he said quietly, and she felt, almost skeptically.

"What is your line of business, Padrig?" she asked, trying to keep the chatter light.

"My line?" he laughed. "I'm the black sheep of the family. A dabbler, you might say. Searching for the big pot of gold from one of the little people." He threw her a quick glance. "I almost had it once or twice, but . . ." his voice trailed off as if pondering what he had just said.

"You don't really believe in them, do you—the little people I mean?" she laughed.

"Oh? The leprechauns? Of course I do. I told you, I almost caught one of the little rascals a few times. Had him by the collar, I did, after snatching him away from his shoemaking work."

"Well, what went wrong? Did he give you the pot of gold?" She laughed, trying to go along with his fantasy.

"You do know, don't you, that once you catch the little devils, you must not take your eyes off them for one instance, or they will disappear. Well, that's happened to me. I let my eyes wander for a few seconds to see if I could spy the gold or the hoarding place for it—they are great hoarders you know—and would you believe it; he was gone in a flash and my hand was clutching onto air."

She looked at him and laughed, and the sight of the serious expression on his face made her laugh even harder.

"You're not believin' me then?" he asked in a thick brogue.

"You believe in luck then?" she smiled.

"Luck, yes, my dear cousin. Luck and a little bit of logical calculation and deep planning," he answered as his face still showed merriment.

She looked over at him and wondered about her newly met relative.

"Come now, cousin. The look on your face is wistful. Did I frighten you with my bantering? Afraid you've come to live with a madman who believes in legends and lives in fantasies?"

"No, nothing like that," she answered.

"This country is full of fantasies," he said. "Look, Terrace. Do you see that field over there?"

Her eyes followed his outstretched hand. "It's so green, everything is so green here."

"Yes, but notice the lone tree standing in the center of the field with the land plowed around it. You see?

The farmer plowed to the tree, didn't disturb it, and plowed around it and continued on after."

"Yes, I see that," she answered.

"Now I'm going to explain this to you so that you won't think I'm the only loony one around here. The farmer, cousin dear, did not disturb the tree because it is a fairy tree—and we Irish do not disturb the lone fairy tree in a field. It would be very unlucky if we did, do you see?"

"I see," she laughed heartily and she saw his face contorted in an expression of extreme mirth.

"No, really, Terrace. This is one of the better-known legends. Look over there at that field," he continued and this time pointed toward the left. "Do you see the circle of bushes in the bare field of grass?"

"Yes," she commented, not knowing what else to expect from him.

"Now that is called a fariy wrath, and that is the place where the little people live. Like the fairy tree, no one would disturb the fairy wrath or enter into the center of it."

They were silent for a few minutes and suddenly his face turned to her and she realized that she had been peering over his shoulder looking at the circle of bushes with a very serious, determined expression on her face. Only his loud guffaw and laughter made her sit back on her side of the car again, mortified at the flush that she knew had crept into her face.

"We've gotten ourselves a little innocent one," he continued guffawing.

"Cousin Padrig, you are a rogue," she said quietly but stiffly.

13

"That I am and a little worse," he said, his face sobering a little.

"I'll remember you admitted to that," she answered, refusing to smile.

"I always admit my foibles. I told you that I'm the black sheep of the family. Not to be trusted I am. I'm the first one to warn you of that. But don't hate me for it, cousin. Circumstances have made me this way," he said between laughter.

"What circumstances?" she questioned.

"Oh, too many to bother your little head about. But one thing I will tell you. I'm not a liar—not outright, that is. The fairy tree and the wrath—those are true legends I told you about, handed down over the centuries. Now, believing them is up to the individual."

"And the rest at the house. Are they all like you, Padrig?" she asked which made him laugh even harder.

"No. They are not like me at all. I'm the only one in the household who enjoys life—who knows how to enjoy it. That's why I think it's a good idea that you'll be visiting us. We need more life in the family."

"Tell me about the others, Padrig," she said after a few minutes. "Aunt Agatha only had a vague idea of who would be at the house. And do you know anything about my parents? I know very little about them."

"I remember your mother, Terrace. She was a beauty like yourself. I was about ten when I last saw her here in Dublin . . . I'm that much older than you, you see. I remember seeing you also. You were a mass of copper curls, a very pretty wench—as you are now."

"Tell me about my parents, Padrig," she pleaded,

disregarding his flattery. "Aunt Agatha could tell me so little about their lives."

"I don't think I could tell you very much about them, lass. They were in transit a lot, and I being the age that I was knew very little about them since they were not permanent members of the household after I came to live there. Of course, Moira could tell you more . . . if she weren't so sick. If and when she recovers, I'm sure she would be a good source of information to you," he answered and then became silent as if he were through with the conversation.

"But surely you could tell me more about the people who are part of the household now?"

"That I can. No trouble with that at all. As I said, there's Moira, your father's sister and our aunt who is partially paralyzed and lost her speech completely. The house is hers, as she is the eldest living member of the family. That fact, dear cousin, bothers my mother, Pegeen, very badly. She'd like a piece of that house, she would, but she is made to suffer for her irresponsible ways of the past."

"What do you mean?" she asked, surprised that he would speak in such a way about his own parent.

"Oh, nothing that terrible in cosmopolitan circles. But . . . my mother left home to marry someone from Marseilles—a terrible thing to do to a prominent Irish family reared on its children marrying their own kind. What made it worse was the fact that the marriage didn't last, and Pegeen had to come crawling back to the big house—as we all refer to it—with a young child, me humble self, in tow."

"How sad for her," she said.

"Oh, but Pegeen mended her ways pretty fast. I always call mother Pegeen, by the way, and it puts her into a rage. Nevertheless, in order to repent for what the family called her foolishness, she became a fanatic to family loyalty and detests outsiders. She'll probably give you a going over for a while until she gets used to you," he laughed. "But I see although you're all feminine and fancy, you've got a hard core to you, and I'm sure you'll be able to take it."

"But, Padrig, I wouldn't want to stay at the house if my presence is going to disturb anyone."

"Nonsense. It will be fine, cousin. It will be fine. When Pegeen sees how well you get on with Moira and how helpful you'll be in reading to her and sitting with her, she'll come around."

She looked at the man next to her and for a moment, she was unable to speak.

"What's the matter, cousin? What have I said?" he muttered.

"I think we'd better reestablish why I'm here, Padrig. I don't intend to snub the members of the household, but I am here on holiday. I don't think I'll be spending all my time within the house."

"Oh, I know, you'll want to see the sights. I'll show you all the historical points in two days," he said flippantly.

"Padrig!"

"You have to understand, Terrace, that we desperately need something new to happen in our family. It used to be such a social family, with many parties and lots of contacts. We've lost all that, you see."

"And how am I to bring the family back to what it was?" she asked quietly.

"I'm not sure," he answered. "But the fact that

someone new will be staying with us makes me very happy indeed. It will relieve my mother from a lot of tasks in running the house. Perhaps then she will regain the composure she used to have and the family will take its place in prominent society again. We've even lost our cook . . . can't afford to replace her," he said, looking at her from the corner of his eye. "And, if you could help with Moira, you'll be replacing the chores that Kevin's wife did."

"Who is this Kevin? Another cousin?"

"Only by marriage. His wife, Nora, was a Connors—a second cousin. She was a nurse and very close to Moira when she was a child and when they heard of her illness both Nora and Kevin came running here. Nora was great with Moira. They even had some way of communicating with each other, or so Nora claimed. Then poor Nora was killed off the cliffs off Howth. Kevin was always a serious chap. Had some business problems and spent the last few years trying to straighten them out. They used to travel a lot. He's very morbid now. Never was fond of the chap myself. Too serious for me."

"And that's it, Padrig? Those are the people who will be in the house?"

"Yes, cousin," he said in all seriousness. "Those are the people. And, oh, yes, there's Sheila. She's in and out of Dublin. She works in fashion. After Kevin, I think. But it won't be long until she sees which one of us is better for her. She likes the good things in life."

"When you find the lucky pot of gold, Padrig?" she said sarcastically.

"Well, I'm already on my way being lucky aren't I? You're sitting here about to spend a good bit of time

17

at the house. You never know, cousin. Sometimes one thing starts something else rolling," he winked at her and then concentrated on the road ahead of him, as if he expected no more conversation from her.

She sat back on her side of the car and looked at the curious man next to her, not knowing what to think of him. The lines in his face made him look weathered. Yet, through all of his good sense of humor she wondered if they were formed by worry and constant determined thinking as seemed to be going on now while he drove in silence.

He was a mixture of contrasts, she finally decided. And as her eyes left him and took in a panorama of the land ahead of her, she wondered if Padrig was not anything less than the country he lived in. Not many miles away, she could see the buildings and steeples that were probably her first glimpse of Dublin. Still, for miles before the city, the rolling green terrain was spotted at random with thatched cottages and gray ruins of withered castles.

Padrig Corot seemed to feel that her visit to Dublin would be the cure for a variety of family problems. Yet her only purpose in visiting Ireland was to spend a carefree few weeks before returning to San Francisco to establish herself as an interior decorator.

Padrig would have to be disappointed, she thought. There was no way that she would enter into any family intrigues while on her holiday.

Chapter 2

The house was Georgian in architecture and elegant. It was one of many Georgian homes on Merrion Square, yet it was the largest and the one which would first catch anyone's eye as they approached the area.

When they had reached the outskirts of the city, they seemed to fly through it with Padrig shouting out landmarks—Grafton Street, the Leffy, Trinity College—every few seconds.

"Padrig, I don't consider this ride through town a sightseeing trip," she said firmly. "I expect to visit these places slowly like a proper tourist."

"Of course you will, cousin. I was only trying to be helpful," he answered.

But she realized that he was only trying to be helpful to himself. The fervor of racing through town only showed that Padrig was taking her visit as a cure-all to anything that was ailing the family on Merrion Square.

She sighed deeply as the car began to slacken its pace, realizing that they must be nearing the part of the journey she was dreading the most since she left San Francisco. What would she say to these people who were part of her own bloodline and yet strangers to her?

With the surprise announcement of the trip by Aunt Agatha, she never thought too much about the individual people in the house, or how any of their situations would be affecting her.

"Terrace?" Padrig had been speaking to her as he fully stopped the car now and swung her case between them from the back seat.

"I'm sorry, I . . ."

"Not to worry, cousin. I know exactly how you feel."

"I don't know if you really do, Padrig. I just want to make it clear once and for all that I'm merely here on holiday. I can't take the responsibility of straightening out family problems of which I know nothing. If I'm going to disturb Pegeen or anyone by staying here for a while, I could merely check into a hotel."

"Now, now. You're here to have a good time. Yet, anything you could do to help the family wouldn't be harmful along the way."

"If you have to go through this much trouble to impress Sheila, Padrig, I should think you'd give up and try somewhere else," she said, looking at her cousin through the corner of her eye and realizing that her comment hit home.

"She's worth going through a bit of trouble to get, Terrace. You know, I'm happy we've talked like this. Now I know I have an ally," he said and before she could protest, he opened his door, swung the suitcase out of the car, and indicated that she follow along from the driver's side, which further infuriated her.

There were just three steps up to the main portal, and Padrig was already ahead of her pulling at the bell plunge as the door swung open even before she was up the stairs herself.

"Mr. Padrig," the small girl with fuzzy yellow hair exclaimed.

"Yes, yes, Lizbeth," he answered her with a casual wave of his hand as he beckoned Terrace to follow him with a gesture of his chin. "I am back, Lizbeth, and this is Miss Terrace Connors who will be staying with us for a while."

"Yes, Mr. Padrig," the girl answered, as she smoothed down her starched white apron which almost fully covered an equally stiff-looking black serge dress. At that point, Terrace noticed without reason that the lace collar and cuffs of the girl's dress were made of the finest lace that she had seen in a long while.

"Did you make up one of the guest rooms as I asked you, Lizbeth?"

"Yes, I did do that, sir."

"That's a good girl," he answered as he patted her shoulder. "Now, take Miss Connors up to her room and bring her a good brunch."

"Yes, sir," the girl fluttered.

"Oh, and where is everyone, Lizbeth?"

"I've been up with Miss Moira. Your mother, sir, is out as she usually is at this time of day."

"And Kevin?" he questioned. "Where is Kevin? I want him to meet Miss Connors," he said anxiously.

Terrace bit her lip and took an inward sigh. So that's it, she thought. Good Cousin Terrace, single and twenty-one, has arrived from the States. What an enticing situation to put before Kevin, therefore leaving Sheila free to be wooed by Padrig.

"I have not seen him at all, sir," Lizbeth was answering.

"Well, he should be in soon," her cousin ventured.

"Terrace, after you unpack and have something to eat, I imagine you will want to rest."

"And what time have you programmed me to waken, Mr. Padrig?" she asked him with obvious snideness, unconcerned about how it sounded in front of Lizbeth.

"Now, now, cousin. I just want to make things pleasant for you. I know everything is strange in a new house, and I merely thought you'd like a few suggestions on how to spend your day. We'll be meeting for a sherry hour before dinner and I thought you'd like to look refreshed."

"For whom," she said directly.

"For . . . for all of us, Terrace."

"Well, I'm happy that my schedule will at least include sherry and dinner," she answered.

"This way, miss." Lizbeth seemed to enter at just the right moment to cover the sudden awkwardness between the two cousins and Terrace allowed herself to be led up the large staircase without another word passing between herself and Padrig.

Lizbeth had insisted on carrying her one suitcase and as Terrace rambled after the servant, her eyes took in at a fast glance the entrance hall and all of its fixtures. Although her mind was almost totally on the uncomfortable position her cousin was trying to foist on her, the opulence of the interior of the house, even from a bird's-eye view, made a definite impression on her. It also led her to wonder why a family which seemed well heeled in their grand house and elegant accommodations would find it difficult financially to rehire a cook, as Padrig had mentioned.

They had been walking down a long hallway to the

right of the landing when Lizbeth finally stopped in front of a double doorway of rich mahogany which she pushed open and indicated to Terrace to follow. The sight that caught her eyes made her gasp. If she had thought the entranceway and foyer were attractive, the single bedroom that they had just entered was beyond belief. The tapestry drapes in shades of pale blue and violet matched exactly the canopy top of the grand four poster and the bedspread itself. The carpeting was of the same hue as the blue tones in the tapestry, and the bows on the lace cover of the circular table also picked up this same hue.

"It is lovely, isn't it, Miss Connors?" Lizbeth said in a hushed voice as if in reverence to the surroundings.

"Indeed it is," she answered, a little more sarcastically than she intended. "Are . . . is this typical of the rooms in the house, Lizbeth? I wouldn't want to be shown any preference. I am family, you know."

"Pay it no mind, miss, and enjoy the room. One is just better than the next in elegance. The house is grand, that's what it is, just grand," she chatted as she bustled around fluffing the bedspread and then walking over to open the tall French doors that made up the windows. "You have a small patio outside these doors, miss," she continued, "but your room does face the Square and I'll doubt that you'll be wanting to sun yourself with all the passersby. But it is nice to look up at the stars from the patio late at night when the rest of the houses are dimmed and there is no one to notice you. Of course, we do have a sunning area in back and a lovely garden."

"It all sounds so accommodating," she answered as she eyed the girl and marveled at her enthusiasm.

Then, suddenly, she knew what she was about to do next, hated herself for it, but went ahead anyway. "Yes, it does sound grand. You should be commended over the way you keep up the house, Lizbeth. It's all so clean and tidy and all that is thanks to you, I imagine."

"Oh, I only straighten up each day and that is only in the few rooms which used. I'm mostly here to tend to mistress Moira's needs. Two people come from the Center every Thursday to clean the house thoroughly. And they work from sunup to sundown. It would be too much for me, miss."

"I see," she answered quietly as she sat on a straight-backed chair. "Then when Kevin's wife, Nora, died you were taken off your regular duties of housekeeping and placed in charge of Moira?"

"Oh, no, miss. We've always had the two from the Center to clean. And, miss, my duties were always merely to straighten up and attend to any personal needs of mistress Moira. When Mr. Kevin and his wife arrived, it almost lessened my duties. Mrs. Sanford was always dedicated to the mistress, she was. She had stayed with her for a while as a child and never forgot mistress Moira's kindness. She came immediately after the accident. She was marvelous with the mistress. Such a young and lonely person, she was."

"Well, I still think you're doing a good job, Lizbeth. After all, you lost your cook and I imagine you have to fill in there a lot."

"Oh, I can't take credit for the cooking. Padrig's mother sees to that. She is quite devoted to cooking, she is. Would never let anyone but herself fix the meals. I merely serve the meals, miss. Oh, I do make

24

breakfast for the family. But I've always done that. It's such a small task."

"Yet I imagine the family feels that you're irreplace-able."

"Oh, thank you, miss," the girl flushed. "Now that you'll be about the house, I know mistress Moira will feel very pleased. I know she missed Nora very much. Nora used to say that one could tell all of the mistress's expressions through her eyes. I'm sure her eyes will show nothing but pleasure at the sight of you, Miss Connors."

"Thank you, Lizbeth," she answered quietly, feeling all the more guilty at having pried information out of the girl.

"Should I run your bath now, miss, while I unpack for you?"

"No, don't bother please. I'll do both myself."

"Yes, miss," the girl said hesitantly as if surprised at the other girl's preference to be self-sufficient. "I'll bring you a tray in a short time, as Mr. Padrig suggested."

"All right, Lizbeth. I'll take the tray here in my room," *and keep Padrig happy*, she wanted to add, but kept it as a silent thought.

The young servant left immediately and Terrace sank exhaustedly on the brocaded chaise that was situated near one of the French doors. It seemed that an eternity had passed since she had left Kennedy airport just hours before. Her main concern now was how the family would welcome her. In her excitement over the trip, she failed to give thought to the fact that she would be interrupting a household which had its own schedule and people whose lives had been functioning for years without much knowledge of her own existence. She held tightly to the arms of the chaise as she cringed and thought of the guile of Padrig Corot trying to fit in her stay at the house with his immature problems of the heart. He even tried to impose on her sympathy by saying that her presence in the house would alleviate his mother's chores and responsibilities there.

He already mentioned in the car ride from the airport that he was the odd one in the family, and although she first thought of the statement as humorous, she could well believe it now.

She leaned back and closed her eyes, trying to rest her mind into blank peacefulness for a moment, but the moment would not come. Instead she became more incensed over the fact that her own cousin was trying to match her with Kevin Sanford in order to gain the favor of the mysterious Sheila. No, he had not come directly out with this fact, but calling her an ally of his after she intimated it to him practically confirmed the situation.

And yet, in thinking further, why should she condemn Padrig for his intensity if he were that smitten with the girl? Actually, she should not try to judge anyone in their dealings with love. In looking back, she could never say to her dear cousin Padrig that she knew what he was going through, as she never did go through anything in depth that matched what he seemed to be suffering. In fact, at times, she wondered if she would ever be capable of an intensity of feeling. Her only concern through life seemed to be in keeping the harmonious existence within Aunt Agatha's house and a deep preoccupation not to be a burden to her.

And yet, she did attend all the social functions her classmates had and never missed being invited to a big dance or important party. But her escorts were always good friends rather than emotional attachments. No, she could not say that she was ever near being in love, and now wondered if she would ever allow herself the indulgence of ever being stirred that deeply. She was brought up too practically for the love that Padrig was showing. And yet . . . she envied him in a way. No, she would not fully condemn Padrig for thinking of using her in his complicated games. In fact, she would allow him his antics without getting too personally involved. She would sightsee in Dublin until she had her fill and then move on to another city.

She sighed once again and decided to get to her unpacking and bath before the overefficient Lizbeth returned with her food. She would tell Padrig once more not to depend on her help in his plot to take Sheila from Kevin. And then she would let the matter rest and get on with her holiday.

Suddenly, she stopped in her paces toward the suitcase and looked over at the French doors. No, she couldn't sun herself in front of the passing populace, but she would get a breath of air on the balcony and try to waken her senses after the long plane trip. As she stepped outside, she realized that there was one more floor to the house which might contain extra guest rooms or even a few rooms for the staff. Many of these were probably closed off now. She could understand how Padrig must feel lamenting a past which the physical aspect of the house seemed easily to suggest. She could imagine a slew of servants cleaning and polishing and making things spic and span for a great array of elegant parties and dances that the family offered. She could understand Padrig lamenting all this, as it was probably within his generation that it was all changed and diminished. Yet the house was still impressive, and it was where he could live the rest of his life in comfort, and she thought that at least he should be content with that fact.

She turned, entered her room again, and unpacked the few things from her suitcase with a personal promise to visit one of the shops in town to add to her wardrobe. Then she proceeded to the private adjoining bath that was almost as large as her own bedroom. She knew immediately, without being told, that the room was constructed of imported Portuguese pink marble. The towels and other linens were plush and with deep pile and of a darker dusty pink which matched the hue of the velvety pile carpet.

She was relieved to soak in the hot tub once she had drawn her bath, but although her limbs began to relax, her mind continued racing. She wondered what Pegeen would be like and if Kevin knew what Padrig had in mind for him and the newly arrived house guest. Then she reprimanded herself. Her composure would have to be worked on before she faced the family that evening, she thought. If she were this addled now, she could be in a sorry state by dinnertime if she didn't allow herself to relax and concentrate on why she was there in the first place—and that was to be at leisure.

She dried herself thoroughly and slipped on a thin blue Banlon robe that just reached her thighs. She began to walk over to the closet, thinking of choosing a pair of slacks and top to lounge in on the chaise until dinnertime when the door opened.

The gentleman who stood there was tall with dark wavy hair and large penetrating brown eyes. Their gaze met and held, and her initial shock over the intrusion was stifled by her reaction to the deep sensitivity of the man's face. His eyes left hers for a moment as they traveled down the front of her robe and the length of her legs. Only then did she remember the thin texture of the material in her covering and the fact that every contour of her body must be visible to him from where he stood.

His eyes shot up to meet hers again and with a grimace that showed nothing less than disgust placed his hand on the doorknob. Instead of leaving as she thought, he closed the door and leaned his heavy frame against it.

"Who are you? What are you doing here?" he asked, his voice deep and resounding.

"I'm . . ." she began to cower, and then she tossed back her shoulders, throwing to the wind all care concerning her garb and answered him defiantly. "I'm Terrace Connors. But it's not important to you why I'm here but rather why you chose to enter my room without knocking."

"Connors? Greg Connors's daughter?" he asked, his face showing surprise but not enough to soften the taut features of anger which lined it.

"Yes, my father was Gregory Connors. But you haven't answered my question. What right have you to barge in here?" She lifted her chin and placed her hands on her hips, trying to muster all the agitation that she could in her stance.

29

"The same right, Miss Terrace Connors, that you have in being here. None at all," he bellowed as his gaze went over her again, and this time so much more slowly that she felt her face begin to flush.

"Well, I'll ask you kindly to leave, then," she snapped, trying not to let down her mood.

"And I'll ask you to do the same, Miss Connors," he answered, his eyes blazing.

"Not until I accomplish what I came for, Mr. . . . ?"

"Sanford. Kevin Sanford. And what have you come to accomplish, may I ask?"

"That, Mr. Kevin Sanford, is none of your business," she said slowly, narrowing her eyes as she stared back into his.

There was a moment of silence between them at which time she thought she noticed a look of amusement creep into his darkened expression. But soon his face hardened again.

"What are you doing here anyway, Miss Connors? What are you doing showing up in a family that you cared nothing about all these years?"

"I have as much right to be here as you do."

"Probably more, if we're thinking of rights," he said as if in private thought rather than conversation.

"Then why suggest that I leave?"

There was more silence before he answered. Then, "Because you're not needed here. You're not needed to tend to Moira, as Lizbeth sees nicely to that. And Moira is holding her own nicely, so if you've come to reap from her demise, you'll be disappointed."

"Are you insinuating that I . . . ?"

"And if you're thinking of staying on indefinitely, the family can't carry any more sponges. Padrig has

30

played that role out to the limits and there's no room for any more like him in this house. If you're merely on a visit, one or two days will do. Why not go to the Continent . . . Paris. You would like Paris," he said as he glanced again at her scanty covering.

"I have no intention of going to Paris. And I will stay as long as I like in Dublin."

He looked at her for a long moment, his face suddenly losing its anger and becoming quiet and somewhat somber.

"As you wish, then," he said quietly and turned to reopen the door. Before passing through, he looked back at her and said, "Oh, by the way, Miss Connors," and here he paused to look over her scanty attire once again and added, "We usually dress for dinner in this house."

Chapter 3

Her dreams were varied, loosely connected and quite childish. Initially, she saw Padrig sitting atop a large golden caldron leaning to one side and then another, chuckling and howling and chanting that he had found the pot of gold that was his and no one else's. Then the scene changed to Kevin Sanford, his face looming dark and sensitive before her eyes. And behind him the image of Aunt Agatha, smiling and chattering and once in a while calling out her niece's name.

When Terrace first sat up in bed, she was confused about her surroundings. She had been panting, and beads of perspiration were rolling down her face from her forehead. Suddenly the present loomed up before her and she knew where she was and that the disconnected scenes were only part of a dream that probably stemmed from an accumulation of emotional exhaustion and travel fatigue.

The sun had disappeared from the shirred curtains on the French doors and she realized she would have to dress and prepare for the meeting with the other members of the family. Her thoughts went immediately to Kevin Sanford and his abrupt intrusion on her privacy hours before. "You've certainly come into an interesting group of them," she said aloud as she rose from the four poster bed and shuddered again at the thought of Kevin.

If she thought she was miffed over Padrig's guile in weaving her into his romantic intrigues, she was no less than incensed over Kevin Sanford's long list of false guesses as to why she was in Dublin.

The shrill ring of the telephone startled her from her reverie as she was about to run a second bath for herself. At first, she could not find the location of the apparatus and finally discovered it resting on a small table partly hidden by the chaise.

She made herself comfortable on the lounge and pulled the table alongside it as she lifted the receiver.

"Terrace? Is that you, Terrace?" came the breathlessness on the other end mixed heavily with transatlantic static.

"Aunt Ag? Oh, Aunt Ag, it's really you," she cried as if it were that very moment when she had awakened from the dream and felt relieved.

"Are you there all right, Terrace?" came the inane but cherished chatter of her aunt.

"Yes, no worse for wear from the trip."

"You sound . . . funny. Are you all right?"

"I was just sleeping, Aunt Ag."

"Sleeping? Well, why Terrace? What's wrong?"

"Nothing's wrong. You must remember that I've come through many different time zones. I was sleeping because I was exhausted from traveling, Ag."

"Oh." Then there was silence. "Terrace, did you . . . did you meet anyone nice on the plane?"

"Yes, Aunt Ag."

"Oh, Terrace. That's just marvelous. What's his name, dear?"

"His name? Oh, no. I meant that all of the crew were very accommodating. One stewardess in particular was very nice. I think she realized that it was my first trip out of the country."

"Well, I didn't mean that, Terrace."

"What did you mean, Aunt Ag?"

"Well, there you are on a foreign holiday and according to all the books and brochures you should meet . . . many people."

"There were a lot of people on the tour I took in New York. But the plane was only half full, and I preferred it that way. Then Padrig met me at the airport and drove me here," she answered slightly confused.

"Padrig? Now who is Padrig, Terrace?"

"Padrig, if you remember, is my first cousin. He's the one who answered my letter to say it was okay to stay at the house."

"Oh," was the older woman's obviously disappointed comment to that.

"Aunt Ag?"

"Yes, Terrace."

"Who exactly do you want me to meet here?"

"Oh, everyone, someone," was her aunt's quick answer.

My God, thought Terrace, I don't believe this. "Aunt Ag, I've only just arrived. I'm sure that my acquaintances will be many by the time the trip is over."

"Who is at the house, Terrace?" her aunt went on as if completely disregarding what Terrace had just said.

"I haven't met all of them yet, Aunt Ag. But there's Padrig . . ."

"Yes, yes, but he's a first cousin."

". . . and then there's Moira, who is an invalid. Pegeen is Padrig's mother. And then there's Kevin."

"Kevin? Another first cousin, Terrace?"

"Well . . . no. He's not really a blood relation at all."

"Well now," her aunt huffed in a way she always did when something pleased her. "I know you'll have a grand time on your holiday, Terrace."

"I know I will," she answered, repressing a childish urge to blurt out, "I know what you're up to," in a singsong voice as she used to do as a child.

"Anything wrong, Terrace?" her aunt asked, obviously catching the sudden tightness in her voice even over the static.

"Nothing is wrong, Aunt Ag. I do intend to have a good holiday. It's only . . . well, I've just arrived, you see."

"Just take your time, Terrace. There's no rush."

"No rush for what, Aunt Ag?"

"Well, to do anything. To meet people and all that. I just want you to remember one thing."

"Yes, Aunt Ag?"

"Try not to dote on me here, or anything in San Francisco. You've been a good niece all these years, always worrying about me. Now it's your time to enjoy yourself."

"I'll remember, Aunt Ag," she said as she heard her aunt click off.

Terrace sat with the receiver to her head, seemingly unconcerned over the buzz that now whirled in her ear.

As she replaced the receiver in its cradle, she had an uncontrollable urge to burst into tears. Good, sweet, overprotective Aunt Agatha had suddenly taken on a new role as matchmaker for her niece. Suddenly Terrace felt that a weight had been lifted from her own shoulders. There had always been some wariness on her part ever since the moment that Agatha had presented the airplane tickets to her. There had been a certain childish delight in her aunt as she talked of her niece's upcoming holiday. And although Terrace first thought that the excitement emanating from her aunt was a result of many years of pennypinching—she now realized that she should have known her aunt better than to think she would do anything without a practical aspect to it.

So Aunt Agatha had finally decided that it was time her niece met someone. Don't think of me or anything about San Francisco, she had said. It was time to enjoy yourself, she had added. Did Aunt Ag really think that she had stifled Terrace all these years, she wondered—and in wondering, she wiped away a single tear that could not be controlled and which started to make its way down her cheek. Poor, silly, wonderful Ag, she thought. And then she chuckled to herself. Now she had both Padrig and Agatha depending upon her during her holiday.

She sighed a very deep and audible sigh and prepared herself as quickly as possible for the reunion with the family.

When Lizbeth finally knocked on her door to summon her downstairs, she had already donned a silk dress with a muted wine and green print against a white background. She knew that the colors highlighted the color of her auburn hair, but she did wonder if the fabric and the aura would be too summerlike for a May evening in Dublin. After fastening a pendant around her neck, she lifted her shawl from the bureau and threw it around her shoulders.

The whirl of voices emanating from the study reached her even before she descended the staircase, and as she took each step hurriedly, realizing her lateness, she tried to match the voices with the faces that she had already met, but had difficulty with this.

There's no getting around it, Terrace Connors, she said to herself. You're very nervous. And why shouldn't you be addled, she continued. You've had a fantastic beginning to a trip that was supposed to be taken for peace and relaxation. First, a rogue of a cousin meets you at the airport and intimates that he has woven you into his affairs of the heart. Then you receive a long distance phone call from Aunt Agatha who insinuates that within twenty-four hours after leaving home, you should have already met the love of your life. And, in the center of all this, a very sensitive, brooding but attractive man walks into your room unannounced and feels that your visit has underlying reasons behind it. Terrace Connors, you just be as addled as you wish. No one deserves the condition more than you!

It was in this frame of mind that she entered the study, and because of it the faces in the room appeared as a blur of indistinguishable color to her. Suddenly the blur of color approaching her cleared and Padrig's anxious face loomed up before her.

As he took her elbow he whispered, "Let me take the lead—you just follow along," which immediately sent splinters of anger through her body. And these, puncturing the little areas of cowardice that were spread through her, permitted her a bit of composure, as she finally stood in the center of the room surrounded by eyes.

"I know you'll agree with me," Padrig was saying, "in thinking this a most welcome happening. May I present my American cousin who will be spending her holiday with us. A brightening to the house, I'm sure you'll agree."

There was no answer from any of them as they held their faces uplifted in her direction. The moment was grueling but short, as Padrig filled it quickly with a nervous cough and continued.

"May I introduce you, Terrace, to the family. This is my mother, Pegeen Corot." He waited until Terrace extended her hand and smiled at the woman who sat very close to where she was standing. "And at the bar is Kevin Sanford—sorry Sheila, I thought I'd get the family over with first," he said quickly to another girl who sat near the darkened hearth.

"Yes, Miss Connors and I ran into each other before dinner," Kevin said. "She already mentioned that she's here for two days before traveling to . . . was it Paris, Miss Connors?"

"Please call me Terrace," was all she answered as she simultaneously tried to avoid a chuckle. Thinking that this hostile man had already been chosen by Padrig and Aunt Ag as her romantic interest—as well as trying to fend off Padrig's shocked glance at hearing she might leave for Paris—suddenly amused her.

"Oh?" her cousin stammered. "We'll have to do something to change her mind. We can't have this pretty sight leaving after only two days with us, now can we, Kevin?"

"Well, that depends on Terrace I should think,"

Kevin said as he looked down at the drink he was mixing.

"And this, Terrace, is Sheila Malloy. Not family, but as close to it as possible, eh, Sheila?" he quipped.

"Welcome to Dublin, Terrace," the girl said as she rose from her seat and extended her hand in a hearty shake. As Terrace extended her own hand, she noticed that the other girl was dressed in a neat amber tweed jacket and skirt that were impeccably tailored and whose matching amber cashmere sweater showed an equally trim but feminine figure. "Now, Padrig," the girl continued, "leave your poor cousin alone and have her travel on if she likes. My, she's dressed for sunny Spain in May. She might not be prepared in wardrobe to stay longer than a few days here. You are one to foist your own will on people, Padrig Corot."

It was done beautifully, thought Terrace. An outward extension of friendship and welcome mixed with a cunning female viper's sting—the true depth of which only another woman would detect, yet obvious enough to make her own judgment of style be up for question by the males in the room.

"I'm sure your shops will accommodate me quite well, Sheila, if I decide to stay," she answered quietly with a smile that she directed at Padrig—who in turn sighed in thankfulness.

"What would you like to drink, Terrace?" Pegeen finally asked. "Kevin, would you fix our guest something?" She had been staring at her young niece until then as if the sight of her reminded her of someone else.

"What would you like?" Kevin asked, still not meeting her eyes directly.

"I'll have a . . . sherry, thank you," she answered.

"Now you don't have to drink sherry during the sherry hour, Terrace," Sheila laughed slyly. "The bar does hold other things, you know."

"I'll still have a sherry. It seems the best I could think of to . . . ward off the chill," she answered slowly and deliberately as she made her way over to the bar.

Kevin Sanford stood directly behind the bar area and as Terrace placed herself in front of him, she straightened her shoulders and lifted her chin in pre-warned defiance to anything he might say. Yet, he surprised her and remained silent. He seemed to find something amusing in the sherry he was pouring as his lips pursed as if to stifle a grin.

"It's truly amazing," she heard Pegeen say in the background.

"What is, Mother?" Padrig answered.

"The likeness of this child to her own mother."

Terrace then turned in the direction of Pegeen Corot to say, "Aunt Agatha has mentioned a few times that I resemble Mother."

"Resemble is not the word," Pegeen continued. "You are a mirrored image of Stacey Connors."

"And that should be a compliment to Terrace, isn't that right, Mother?" Padrig asked.

The pause was apparent to Terrace before Pegeen answered drily, "Are you like her in personality also?"

"I don't know really," she said. "I don't remember my mother."

"Well, of course you wouldn't. The accident occurred when you were very little."

"I was almost four," Terrace said.

40

Kevin was handing her the glass of sherry then and his eyes finally lifted from the bar to meet hers. For a moment she felt that his gaze was deeply penetrating, yet almost tender as if he knew what pain the scene in the study was giving her. She felt her face turning a faint scarlet and she was annoyed at herself for giving any inclination to him that he had affected her in that manner. As she took the sherry from him, the movement of her arm released the shawl that had been draped across the front of her shoulders and his eyes went immediately to the low neckline of her dress and the folds of material that were draped snugly across its bodice. Her face turned a deeper scarlet but as he quickly turned away, she hoped that it went unnoticed.

"Come, Terrace, pet, sit here near Mother," Padrig was saying. "Tell us all about yourself."

"Yes, do, Terrace," Sheila quipped. "You live with an old maiden aunt, don't you?"

"I live with my mother's sister," she answered quietly.

"How good of you. Such a sense of family. Most girls your age would have an apartment of their own—especially in the States. She must be endeared to you for keeping house for her instead of . . . making your own life," Sheila said flippantly.

"Aunt Ag keeps her own house," she answered. "I've just finished school and . . ." she checked herself. She was falling into the trap that Sheila had set for her—defending herself from a role that the other young girl had created for her. "I enjoy Aunt Agatha. I've had a good life living with her and I don't think I'd change it for a moment."

"Of course not, pet," Padrig stammered as if he suddenly realized the battle going on between the two young women.

"Terrace, if you really are traveling on to Paris, I could take you over there myself," Sheila continued. "I'll be going in two days on business. I'm a fashion coordinator—or has Padrig mentioned that to you already?"

"No . . . no one has mentioned you at all," she answered flatly.

"I see. Well, if you need someone to travel with, I'll be happy to accommodate you, dear. I make frequent trips to the Continent," she said as she crossed her slim legs and reached for a cigarette.

"I'm not sure what my plans will be at this moment," she answered. "But I think if I made my way across one continent and a very large ocean, I'll be able to reach Paris without too much mishap."

Sheila chose not to answer, but instead lifted her arm dramatically in Kevin Sanford's direction and said, "Kevin, darling, do come and sit with us. Perhaps you will be my traveling companion again the next time I go to Paris. That was marvelous three months ago when we were able to make the trip together. Tell this dear child what a marvelous traveling companion I make," she chuckled as he walked over to her and sat on the straight-backed chair near the sofa.

Padrig gave Kevin no time to answer and thus annoyed Terrace. "Mother," he said, "I've invited a few people over tomorrow, sort of a welcome party for Terrace. A few of my friends, and I've asked the O'Briens and if you'd like, we'll ring up the Caseys and the Boylans."

"Padrig, how could you think of doing a last-minute thing like that with all that's going on here—Moira and—well . . . everything."

"Mother, we need some life in this house. Moira will never recover fully and . . . we can't just stop existing because we've had a few tragedies. Life must go on. And, besides," and here his sense of humor began to come through again, "we can't have my American cousin thinking we're dowdy."

"Dowdy isn't the word. This family has had enough bad luck to keep us in mourning for the rest of our lives."

"That's just it. Now is the time to break away from living in our miseries. I'll call the Caseys and Boylans then?"

"Since the rest of them are coming," she sighed, "I guess we can't leave them out."

"That's marvelous."

"Nothing is marvelous about it. Still, we must organize preparations if this party is really to happen."

Terrace sat back in her seat and sipped her sherry quietly, allowing the rest of them to talk of preparations for the coming reception. She took those few minutes to study the people in the room. Her aunt Pegeen interested her. She was at least in her early sixties, a very handsome woman with a rounded Botticelli figure and displaying both efficiency and reluctance which all the more enhanced her femininity. Her aunt and Padrig were doing most of the planning, being interrupted occasionally by the slick personality of Sheila Malloy who tossed her shoulders and her hair every time she spoke—all giving her a provocative and worldly aura. Her black hair reached her shoul-

43

ders and set against the cream tone of her skin, empha-
sized her attractiveness. Now as her eyes moved toward
Kevin Sanford to see if he were being fully taken in by
Sheila's antics, Terrace was shocked to find his eyes
staring directly at her instead, his expression both curious and amused.

She looked down at her drink, praying that the evening would soon be over when Lizbeth came to the
door to announce dinner.

Sheila immediately stood up and placed her arm
through Kevin's while Padrig, seeing this, immediately
swooped over to Terrace and almost plucked her out
of her chair. "Kevin," he said as he led his cousin almost out of the study. "Would you also escort Mother,
while I lead our new guest?"

"Certainly," Kevin answered, still seeming in an
amused state.

"Padrig, you seem to have won out on the party.
Still, from my standpoint, you're batting zero with
Sheila," Terrace said.

"Not to worry, cousin, not to worry. It's just that
I'm madly in love with Sheila, and she in turn with
Kevin. I thought some distraction and new activity in
the house might give me some time."

"I think you're going to need more than my presence as a plan of action," she said.

In looking over at her cousin who decided to remain
silent, and noticing the light film of perspiration on
his face, she realized that if the evening seemed long
and uncomfortable to her, Padrig Corot was having an
even more difficult time of it.

Chapter 4

The drapes were parted just centimeters, and the early morning sunrays, playing no favoritism in their late spring strength, hit directly on her eyelids and made her wince and scowl and then open her eyes completely. The change of time zones had finally gotten to her and she had slept exhaustedly once her head had reached the pillow. The double mattress had been just firm enough to rest her body comfortably and yet soft enough to give her the feeling of luxury. The down-filled satin quilt added to this feeling of elegance and she had allowed herself to sink deeply into an undisturbed slumber.

Much of her exhaustion, she knew, stemmed from her emotional state the evening before. It had been enough to fend off Sheila's snippy remarks. But what really had stung her was the obvious negative attitude of Kevin Sanford. Why he should greet her arrival as anything devious was beyond her comprehension. In thinking it over now she realized how different her reception had been from each of the men. Padrig had been full of good cheer, ready to make her arrival into an opportunity for himself. Yet he was willing to use her visit in a positive manner—even if it were egocentrically contrived. But Kevin had found her arrival almost threatening. He had thought that her visit was timed with her aunt's ill health—waiting for her demise—he had said. How could he? How could he even *insinuate* that she might be there to reap from her aunt's passing? And yet what else could he think about a blood relative who had not even exchanged greeting cards for almost two decades only to ascend upon the house on Merrion Square when Aunt Moira was gravely ill. What else could Kevin think, yet Padrig hadn't thought in that vein at all. If it were some inopportune time to visit the family, then Padrig and Pegeen as well as Lizbeth should have greeted her with one eyelid raised for her lack of propriety. But none of the others had shown any suspicions along this line. Oh, yes, Pegeen had been cool and obviously no former fan of Stacey Connors's. And Sheila—well Sheila was altogether another matter. Therefore, it was only Kevin who thought of her arrival as an intrusion for personal gain.

He was a brooding man, brooding and troubled and attractive. She felt her face flush as she stretched herself over to the other side of the bed to languish in the coolness of the yet untouched bedclothes. Nonsense, why should she think a ridiculous thing like that. He was rude and bad tempered. Still, her mind ran quickly to the day before and his unannounced entrance into her room. She remembered the way he had looked at her—at first with curiosity, then with contempt, and finally with definite amusement. And through it all she felt the sadness of his dark eyes and the sensitivity of his mouth. No, Kevin Sanford was not like Padrig at all. Kevin was deep and troubled and . . . and . . . no, Terrace Connors. There will be no more of this.

She lifted the pillows and pushed her head beneath

them as if to block out any further passage of thought from her mind.

She would have to make the best of it, she almost said aloud. She wouldn't blame any of them for being cool in some way to her. Aunt Ag—oh, poor Aunt Ag—had not known "the other side of the family" at all when Terrace was left in her care. At her parents' death, Aunt Ag was in such shock she could barely keep both of them going for the first few years. "Terrace," she had said, "I was scared those first years, scared silly. Not having been married and not having experienced caring for a child of my own, I didn't really know if I could do it. But there you were. Your parents on vacation and you left in my care—and suddenly their accident. There was no choice but to carry on."

And so she had carried on. And once in a while Terrace could remember hearing Aunt Ag remind herself to get in touch with "the others who lived in Dublin," but Aunt Ag never had. At first it was merely that Aunt Ag had had no time. And then Terrace soon realized that Aunt Ag felt if she contacted them after their obvious silence they might feel that she was "looking for something"—as Aunt Ag used to put it.

Terrace pulled her head out from under the pillows and tossed off the mounds of covers. The spell had been broken and sleep had passed. She walked over to the French windows and she could see that the sun was now shining brightly over one part of Dublin while gray and black clouds whirled in a frenzy of wind over the other part of the city. The varied weather of Ireland, she thought. She knew that she had read about it somewhere. And now she was right in the midst of it. Still finding it hard to believe that she was there at all, she dressed in a heavy coffee linen suit and champagne blouse and made her way down to the dining-room for breakfast.

Kevin's large square frame was quickly discernable even before she was fully into the room. His back was toward her as he busied himself at the buffet filling his plate with the delicacies whose aroma now filled her nostrils. Having heard someone enter, he turned slightly and there was a pleasant smile on his face brightening his features in a most attractive manner. The grin faded immediately as he noticed her, however, and he turned back to fill his cup with the dark coffee.

"Good morning," she said cheerily after sighing inwardly and making a personal pact with herself to see this through pleasantly.

"Miss Connors," he nodded as he transported his dish and coffee cup over to one of the places set at the long mahogany table.

"Oh, you must call me Terrace. We are related in some way, aren't we?" she asked as she scooped up a hearty portion of the kidney omelet and rich thick bacon from the serving platter.

"No. We're not related at all," he said looking down into his food as he ate.

"I thought we were cousins," she said, pouring herself a cup of coffee and eyeing the hashed brown potatoes she thought might eventually tempt her.

"Not in the least. I . . . my late wife would have been a very distant cousin of yours. But you and I have no family ties other than that," he answered quietly and in a manner that showed she was invading his privacy.

She paused before choosing a seat, at first thinking that she might choose the place set just next to his, but then decided to sit at the far end of the table instead. She felt she would not have her first full breakfast in Dublin ruined by that morose and ill-mannered gentleman.

As she began to eat, her eyes focused on her silent companion and she was able to do this freely, as he never looked up to pay her any further notice. He seemed to be in his mid-thirties and his face was square and quite attractive, but not as much as it appeared to be when she had caught him smiling as she first entered the room. He was massive and tall, and the more she eyed him the more she felt pangs of hurt that he seemed to relish being rude to her.

Then from boredom, or an increase in her anger over his actions or lack of them, she decided to learn more about him.

"Are you from Dublin proper?" she asked and realized that her voice shook slightly as if from shyness.

He took a while before answering, and then did so reluctantly.

"No, I'm not."

"But you are from Ireland, aren't you?"

Again he hesitated and then said, "Actually I was born in the States."

"You're American?" She was surprised, though she had detected less of an accent from him than from Padrig.

"I only lived there until I was seven," he said. "My parents were Irish."

"I see," she said, and then remained silent as she felt that her interest in him had been too apparent by her schoolgirl questioning.

"Have you seen Padrig around?" she asked, trying to keep things general.

"Padrig?" he echoed and practically stared her into the ground.

"Why, yes."

"Let me give you a word of warning, Miss Connors."

"Terrace," she snapped.

"Don't ally yourself too closely with that one."

"And why not, may I ask?" she said as she realized she was losing her temper rapidly and this showed clearly in the abrupt manner that she spoke.

"He may be your first cousin, but most of his life he's been up to no good, getting into one mishap after another. Most of the funds of this family have gone to bailing out Padrig Corot from his escapades."

"And with whom should I ally myself in his stead then? With you, Kevin Sanford—you who have been most courteous and welcoming since my arrival?"

"You should ally yourself with no one, Terrace Connors. I don't know what you're really after on this visit of yours."

"I've come for a simple holiday, and while I'm here, I intend to spend some time with my aunt."

"And you shouldn't be here annoying her either—hovering in her room and pestering her. Lizbeth knows how to care for her. You'll only be a nuisance loitering around the sickroom."

Sheila Malloy must have had a sixth sense in saving Kevin Sanford from a terrible fate, she thought, as the other girl entered just as Terrace was about to allow her anger to really explode.

"Well, good morning Kevin, darling," she said as she patted his shoulder affectionately.

"Good morning, Sheila," he answered, covering his own angry expression by a wide and very handsome smile. "My, you look attractive this morning," he added and kept attention on the girl who gave him a sly smile as she walked over to the buffet.

"And Terrace, dear. So you have survived the first night in Dublin. Homesick at all?" she asked condescendingly over her shoulder.

"No. Everything is so comfortable and everyone so friendly, how can I long for home?" she said, showing a wide smile of her own.

"Tell me, Terrace," Sheila continued as she set her scantily filled plate down at a place equally distant from the other two. "What will you be doing with this interior design background of yours?"

"Well, eventually I'd like to start my own business with it. I find it very fulfilling. I love to live vicariously while decorating other people's apartments."

"Yes . . . I imagine that would mean a lot to you. Hmm, I must commend Lizbeth. This breakfast is superb."

There it was again, thought Terrace. The serpent's bite, insinuating that she had no life of her own.

"Are you all set for the party, Terrace?" The other girl was still speaking. "Or may I help you get some clothes together? We're about each other's size, you know."

"But that's where the similarity ends, I think, don't you, Sheila? I'm sure I'll be all right."

They were both looking at her now, Sheila in shocked dismay at the sweet little nothing defending herself, and Kevin—she couldn't read his expression exactly. Amused that she had spoken up to Sheila, or delighted that Sheila had been able to embarrass her again. Whatever it was, his face had softened with interest. If she had allowed him to continue staring at her, she would have turned a clear scarlet, for although he had been abrupt and ill mannered since they had first met, it had not lessened his appeal as a very attractive and compelling man.

Sheila quickly rose from the table to pour herself another cup of coffee from the buffet.

"I'll be going into the Center, if anyone wants a lift," Kevin was saying.

"I wish I could go with you," Sheila answered, "but I have some paperwork to catch up on before my meeting with Casey's Boutique. They're doing a large fashion show at Connolly Manor in two weeks and the coordination of it is grueling."

"I'll see everyone at the reception then," he said.

"Have a good day, Kevin," she heard Sheila drawl as she delayed pouring cream into her cup. When she finally turned toward her seat, Kevin was gone from the room and Sheila was eyeing Terrace openly.

"He is quite attractive, don't you think, Terrace?"

"Is he?" she answered.

"Oh, come now, even you have felt his charm."

"Even I?" she repeated with emphasis on the first word.

"Well, you know what I mean."

"No, I don't think so. You tell me."

52

"I only meant that you are quite young to have much experience in the affairs of the heart. But, even so, I've seen you looking at Kevin and I know you think he's attractive."

"I'm a little different than you are, Sheila. I think attractiveness comes from within. I don't know Kevin Sanford well enough to have that type of opinion about him."

"Well, if you do or not, I just want to warn you of one thing. Kevin and I . . . well—we have an understanding."

"Are you formally engaged to be married?" she asked quietly.

"Ah, no, not exactly."

"Then I think you should know something right from this moment. I have no designs on Kevin Sanford. But if I do get any, I'm not going to ask your permission to follow through on them."

"Well, well. So the little mouse shows her true colors as a full grown rodent."

"Only to ward off once and for all any further verbal attacks by a sharp-toothed tigress."

"I really must get back to work," Sheila said as she sipped the last of her coffee and stood up to leave. "Have a good day, dear. And do be careful of the pookas, white horses, banshees, and the lot. Padrig claims you're interested in that sort of thing. Is that true?"

"Not really. Evil only concerns me when it comes in human form."

"Oh, yes. Well, the banshee and the white horse imply danger, but the pooka is a donkey who plays tricks on a person while doing that person's work. Shame on you, Terrace, you should bone up on your ancient Irish lore." There was no time to answer her as she quickly left the room.

Terrace sank back in her seat and just stared at the doorway where Sheila had just exited. Well, chalk up one more enemy, she thought. She was batting a thousand with the household. Actually Pegeen had not given her any trouble yet, but then they had not seen each other very much. She was sure that Pegeen would hold no love for her—having been intruded upon by a long-shot relative.

Terrace sighed as she thought of Sheila again. She might be two or three years older than Terrace, but she had the annoying habit of talking to her as if she were addressing an awkward teen-ager. Of course, Terrace realized Sheila was doing this for Kevin's benefit. So they had an understanding. Well, they could have each other, Terrace agreed as she left the dining room. Yet she was uncomfortable about the fact that her mind kept focusing on Kevin nevertheless.

Lizbeth was a welcome sight as she strutted down the steps all starched and pressed. At least she could speak to Lizbeth without a barrage of snideness being returned.

"Miss Connors, good morning to you," the girl said cheerily.

"Good morning, Lizbeth. I was just off to seek you out. I wonder if I may visit my aunt for a short time?"

"Ah, yes, miss. This would be a good time to visit her. She has had breakfast and a good night's sleep, and I know it would do her a world of good to see you."

"Where is her room located?"

"I'll take you up, miss. It's at the end of the corridor to the left of the stairway. Come, just follow me."

She watched the servant as she followed her up the staircase and marveled at her air of efficiency. She did not wonder that Lizbeth was able to keep the entire household in order and take excellent care of Moira as well. The girl seemed delighted with her score of responsibilities.

"Lizbeth," she asked just before reaching the doorway of Moira's room. "Does she . . . does she know that I'm here?"

"Yes, I already mentioned it to her, miss. I felt it would be too much of a shock for her to see you without some warning. She was so close to your father and took his passing quite hard."

"You knew my father, Lizbeth?"

"Not well, miss. He and your mother were in and out of the place too much for that. Of course, I was a lot younger . . . I'm only a few years older than you are myself. I used to help my aunt when she had duty here."

They had reached the door and Lizbeth opened it swiftly giving Terrace no further opportunity to question her.

The area they first entered was a small sitting room, decorated in various hues of gold and with the brown mahogany furniture gave the aura of being fit for royalty. Lizbeth did not tarry in the area at all and beckoned Terrace to follow her into the adjoining room which opened into a magnificent bedroom still carrying forth the gold theme, but here coupling that with rich tones of beige and brown. The room centered upon a huge canopy bed with three steps leading up to it.

"This is grand, isn't it, miss? I mentioned how marvelous the house was, didn't I?"

"It certainly is magnificent, Lizbeth," Terrace answered casually while all her attention focused on the silver-haired figure that lay in the center of the bed, propped up slightly by two lace-trimmed satin pillows.

"Mistress Moira." Lizbeth had reached the bed a little before Terrace. "Mistress Moira, look what we have here. A pretty young miss has come a long distance to call on you and she is a sight to behold, she is. I'm sure you'll be happy to see such a lovely face as hers."

Lizbeth was being so accommodating and helpful that Terrace only then realized the amount of unfriendliness she had been subjected to until that point. She swallowed hard, marveling at the sudden emotional state she had fallen into, and mounted the steps to the bedside.

"Aunt Moira. It's good to see you. I'm Terrace, your brother Gregory's daughter." She noticed that the woman's eyes widened as she looked directly into her face. "I know, aunt, I look very much like my mother. I didn't know how much until I arrived here. Aunt Agatha, that's my mother's sister, always told me that I resembled my mother a little. But according to Pegeen, I look a lot more like her than I thought."

The woman's eyes never left the girl's face, as if every moment brought back flashes of another time. Suddenly Terrace felt the strain that her presence was taking on the older woman and she wondered if she had erred in visiting her.

"I know, Aunt Moira," she said. "My visit is bound to bring back memories. Only I hope it will bring back the good ones."

The woman continued to stare at her, and as she did so, Terrace noticed that one or two of her aunt's fingers that were previously clasped on the blanket in front of her began to move pointing upward from the rest of the fingers.

She patted the woman's hands then with both of her own, trying to relax them.

"You should rest now, Aunt Moira. But I'll return to visit you again."

The tears that began to stream out of the corners of the woman's eyes startled her.

"Oh, please don't be upset, Aunt Moira. I don't want my presence to make you unhappy."

"Now it doesn't at all, miss," Lizbeth, who had stood silently by until then, suddenly broke in. "Mistress Moira is merely lamenting the fact that she can't speak to you properly. Come, miss, we'll let her rest now. You go on and I'll freshen up her pillows a bit," the girl continued, regaining her efficiency once again.

Terrace walked slowly out of the bedroom throwing one last furtive glance over her shoulder in the direction of her aunt. She realized Moira would be surprised to see her, but she was upset at the final look in her eyes and the tears that poured out afterward.

It was with this worry that she entered the sitting area to the suite, and because of it the sight of Kevin Sanford was more upsetting than usual.

Chapter 5

His hands were carelessly pulling against the black-and-white tweed pockets of his jacket as his body slouched in a nonchalant fashion against the carved outer door to the suite. Yet his face showed an expression that was anything but casual.

She stopped abruptly in her paces when she saw him and then they stared at each other, his eyes blazing with accusation, at what she could not imagine. They would go at it again, she thought—ripping at each other in a battle that had no origin in her capacity of thought. How long would they be playing the game, she wondered.

"I thought you ventured into the center of town," she said.

"I imagine you did," he barely allowed the words to come through his lips that were now pursed in tight antagonism.

"And what does that mean? I've done nothing behind your back."

"I'd say you have," he said, releasing his stance from the heavy door and walking to the other end of the room.

"And what do you think I've done? I merely visited my aunt. What is wrong with that may I ask?"

"The same thing that's wrong with your entire visit

58

here. Why are you here anyway? For personal gain? To stir up trouble?"

"I don't know what you mean," she said, her voice catching just enough to make him turn quickly and look in her direction.

His brows furrowed for a minute and she saw his face soften as if he might believe her. She felt a flush of claret seep across her face, and she bit her lip in an attempt to control it. His own face was troubled and yet quite handsome and she realized that the magnitude of his masculinity could affect her very easily. Yet she despised him, and would not let this happen.

The moment of softness in his features was short lived, however, and he answered snidely, "Don't tell me that you are merely here to vacation and nothing more." He deliberately leaned his body backward to take an obvious look at her from head to toe.

"What else do you think I'm here for, Kevin Sanford? I didn't know the gravity of Moira's illness, so I'm not here waiting to collect on the house. And in that same vein, I could ask why you are still here. You came with Nora when she wanted to care for Moira, I've heard. Now Nora is gone and you're still here. Could it be you're waiting for the same thing you're accusing me of—a part of the estate?" She was sorry for the words as soon as they crossed her lips, but she could do nothing about it then. And the guilt and realization of what she had said acted in reverse and prompted her tongue to become more venomous. "Or perhaps you're resenting the fact that I may be taking Nora's place with Moira. Is that what has prompted you to continue berating me every time our paths cross? Well, let me tell you, Kevin Sanford, I'm not here to take anyone's place or to take anything from this house. But I'll not have you telling me what I can and cannot do here."

His face had gone sallow and she knew she had hurt him deeply. His eyes held hers for a long moment of silent fury and then he did something that she could not understand. He allowed his features to break into a wide grin, as broad as the one he offered Sheila a short while before. And although his eyes remained troubled and weary, the grin was nothing but genuine.

"Welcome to Merrion Square, Greg Connors's daughter," was all he said as he turned from her and left the suite.

She sank heavily into the gold brocade chair and fought unsuccessfully against the stream of tears that lined her face. There was no choice left for her now but to plan on leaving the house and find a place to stay at some hotel. Or perhaps she should leave Dublin completely and head for home. But what good would that do, and which of them would even care? Except Padrig—Padrig would surely care if she left. Yet his upset would be nothing altruistic—only a personal and selfish regret of losing someone whom he had unconsciously enlisted to help him carry out his ridiculous charade of the heart. And then there was the realization that aside from all the snideness she'd been given, she was in her father's birthplace for the first time in her life, and merely being within the same walls where he had played as a child had given her a feeling of closeness to the man whom she could hardly remember. Still, was this enough to keep her there? What pleasures had she given anyone by her arrival?

Even Moira had shed tears at the sight of her. Were they tears of joy at seeing her? She doubted it. Moira had opened her eyes wide when she had first entered the room and at first the expression in those eyes were of happiness. But the joy had lasted only a short while—and then the tears. Was it nostalgia over her dead parents? Perhaps, and yet there were tears. Tears from Moira, anger from Kevin, resentment and jealousy from Sheila and secretiveness from Padrig. Padrig, who had been as nervous as a cat since their arrival from the airport. No, she could not stay the summer. But since she was there, she would visit Moira a few more days and see some of the city, but that would be about the limit of her endurance. In fact, the house seemed to stifle her even now. She would get her wrap and take a walk and in this way rest her mind from the family.

She was pleased at her forethought to add an extra sweater under her trench coat, as the wind blew a mighty gust as soon as she closed the heavy front doors of the house. And yet the sting of the wind piercing and stirring the sun-drenched air seemed to affect her like a cold shower and she realized that she greatly needed a reprieve from the house for a few hours. She was only a few paces on her way when she turned the corner and was confronted by a large stone edifice which bore the name of the National Gallery of Art. She hesitated, knowing that it housed an excellent collection of paintings from the Irish school as well as representation of all leading schools, but she could not make herself enter. She needed the freshness of the air and she promised herself to return to the gallery at another time. Soon there were other buildings that she

61

passed, the glass-walled structure that housed the Department of Welfare, the Municipal Gallery of Modern Art which was actually a magnificent mansion, and St. Michan's Church which she knew contained the eighteenth-century organ once played by the great Handel. She hesitated in front of all of these, yet there was a compulsion in her that made her continue to walk, perhaps to compensate for and to dissipate the turmoil that she felt inside of her.

Finally, she reached the Liffey River and leaned against a railing as she viewed the bustle of O'Connell Street behind her with its double-decked buses and brick-and-stone office buildings and shops. She sighed, thankful to be lost in the anonymity of strangers whose lives affected her in no way. She walked across O'Connell Bridge and joined the throngs browsing in shop windows and gaping at the wares which ran from heavy durable tweeds and fine lace-trimmed linen to Waterford glass, briar pipes and beautiful shillelagh walking sticks.

A corner store with an extensive display of parchments, plaques, and shields, each with a different heraldic crest bearing a prominent family name caught her eye. She wondered if she were to inquire within whether she could get a quick rundown of her family tree that might help her know more about her parents. Of course the proprietor would only tell her about her great, great grandparents, and although her own father would be mentioned with his date of birth, no personal information would be noted in any of the heraldic listings. It would be the family who remained at the house on Merrion Square who could tell her more about her parents. And yet they had not even come around to civil chitchat, much less filling her in on personal family matters.

She was sorry that she had allowed her mind to drift to them again. But how could she help it? She would not be in Dublin at all if it weren't for the people on Merrion Square. And she could not be standing on O'Connell Street now if she hadn't acted so beastly to Kevin Sanford. She blushed as she thought of his dark eyes penetrating her own and of his total gaze as he allowed himself to scan her from head to toe. Still, as she colored, she felt the anger flood through her veins as she thought of his cryptic remarks and nasty insinuations.

She took a deep and audible sigh and was thankful that no one else had stopped to look into the shop window at the heraldic crests. As she sighed her head turned and she saw the awning of the Gresham Hotel. It was no time before she was seated in the tea lounge, picking at dainty sandwiches made of watercress, cream cheese and olives, cucumbers and pâté.

The tea had warmed her and her mind was at ease as she stepped again onto the sidewalk intending to spend another hour browsing along O'Connell Street. Her momentary feeling of contentment was so great that although she heard the voice behind her and realized its familiar ring, she did not stop until it repeated its greeting.

"I said, did you have a good lunch, cousin?"

She turned slowly and only then realized that the first greeting was directed at her.

"Padrig, what are you doing here?"

"How do you like our shops? The one showing the heraldic crests is always interesting to visitors. They work hand-in-hand with Dublin Castle and the record room there. They give nothing but authentic information on family histories."

"But I was looking in that window before I stopped for tea," she cried exasperatedly. "Padrig, have you been following me?"

"That I have. And I've a right to. Who, more than I, should feel responsible for you, lass?"

"But I didn't take off on a dangerous excursion, merely a short trip to the Center. Come, now, Padrig, I don't look as naive as all that?"

"Naive, no. But you are a stranger here, and I do know my responsibility."

"Your responsibility toward whom, Padrig?" and she raised her eyebrow deliberately. Certainly he wasn't being responsible for her, but instead to some prankish whim that he had contrived.

"Now cousin, cousin dear. I really wasn't following you, not at all. I wanted to . . . well, frankly, I wanted to speak to you away from the house."

"Now what would you want to talk to me about that couldn't be said there?" she asked and she was aware of the fact that her voice was high with agitation.

"Hush now, cousin, come along. Let's walk as we chat," he said as he took her arm firmly in his hand and led her along the sidewalk.

"Well, what is it, Padrig? What's so important?"

"I a . . . well it's just that . . ."

"Padrig Corot! I never would have believed it. You're stuck for words, is that it?"

"Not really. It's all very simple when I think about it, yet when I try to put it into words, I . . . well . . .

64

anyway, all I was trying to say is . . . I don't think you're trying very hard."

"At what may I ask?" and she turned her head to see the familiar film of perspiration covering her cousin's face.

"With Kevin, I mean. You could help me out a little if you really wanted to, I should think."

"There, Padrig. You've hit on the basis to the whole thing."

"Have I now," he said, preening prematurely.

"The important part of the matter is that I don't want to help you."

"Now, cousin," he pouted. "What type of talk is that?"

"Padrig, once and for all, I'm not about to get involved with any of your intrigues. As a matter of fact, I don't intend to get involved with any family problems. I'm here on holiday, remember?"

"Yes, cousin dear, I remember," he said sulking.

"And besides, what is so important about Sheila Malloy for you to suffer so much?"

"Ah, Terrace. Sheila is—well, she's lovely. There's a smartness about her that makes a man proud to walk beside her. She has beauty and talent and . . ."

"And money," she added.

"I didn't say that now, Terrace."

"But that's all part of it, isn't it, Padrig."

"Well . . ." he stammered. "I'm not going to be upset about the fact that she's not indigent."

"And Kevin, Padrig? Is he taken in by these same attributes?"

"I can't speak for Kevin. As a matter of fact, I won't speak for Kevin. He's strange, that one. Sulks a lot.

Stays to himself. I think he's brooding over some lost business project. I never did quite know much about him, and don't care to know, mind you."

"And is he intrigued by Sheila's overwhelming beauty, talent, and . . . money also?"

"Can't tell. Perhaps he is," he snapped, but she knew he was not snapping at her but his own miserable plight.

"I imagine once he lost his business, as you say, and then Nora—this last eliminating any claim to the estate, Sheila's money could be as attractive to him as it is to you."

"Now I didn't say that it was her money I was after."

"I know, Padrig," she chuckled. They walked along for a while without speaking, her cousin's hand still clutching at her arm as if grasping at the last remaining straw as a solution to his troubles.

"You know, cousin," he finally said, "we were not always in this predicament. As I already mentioned, the house on Merrion Square was the setting of a great life. We were a prominent family, Terrace. The parties that were given there were lavish. I could remember it all when I was young."

"It was great, the parties were lavish . . . everything from a bygone era. You're living with memories, cousin," she mimicked. "Why don't you forget what the family was and begin again? Perhaps you could raise it back to what it was."

"Oh, it will never again reach those heights."

"Maybe not in the same way, but you could strike out on a new path—feel the accomplishment of your own endeavors. And you'll always have the house. The house is grand. The furnishings are exquisite. There is nothing shabby or bygone about the house."

"Yes, it has remained as it was," he said brightening.

"It still lives up to the family name, Padrig. But, I hope you don't mind my saying that. You're wasting your life looking for a fast highway to your dreams. What would you be interested in—if you had a chance to pursue some area of work?"

"Well, I don't know. I never much thought of it. I went to Trinity for a few years. Studied ancient lore while I was there."

"Ah, now I know why you were able to expound on all those tales riding back from the airport. Fairy tree indeed!"

"Those are called fairy trees, cousin. I swear it."

"You do have a gift of blarney. Perhaps your gift of chatter and sociability should be pursued."

"To which end, cousin?"

"I'm not sure yet, Padrig. I'll think about it, okay?"

"Okay. And in the meantime . . ."

"Yes?"

"Could you . . . do you think you could try to be a little more friendly to Kevin at the party this afternoon? It will be a lovely reception."

And it was, or at least it seemed to be as Terrace first descended the staircase a few hours later. The study was filled with chattering guests, a large number of which spilled easily into the ample entrance foyer and even along the hallway to the back of the house and through a door which she surmised gave access to the garden. The afternoon sun, in a last attempt of strength, came pouring through the windows and its rays lit up the thoughtfully placed bouquets of flowers that seemed to fill the rooms.

As she looked around at the bar area and the abundance of hors d'oeuvres that rested on the exquisite linen tablecloths, she felt pangs of guilt that she had not even offered to help with the preparations. And yet the feelings of guilt were mixed with those of loneliness, as no one had come to her for help either. She nostalgically remembered that she had always been a leading figure in all of Aunt Agatha's get-togethers. And now, as scenes of afternoon teas and Christmas suppers began to float into her mind, she reprimanded herself harshly and started moving among the guests.

Many of the people were Pegeen's age and she guessed that they would be close friends of hers. One or two of these nodded and smiled at her as she passed and one couple who identified themselves as Emma and Joe Boylan surmised who she was and even chatted with her for a few minutes. Still, most of the guests talked among themselves without noticing her.

Her eye soon caught Sheila Malloy whose back was turned in her direction but whose hand gestures and stance easily proved that she was pushing quite heavily in her conversation with Kevin Sanford. The fashion coordinator was dressed in a two-piece silk outfit with a black background and a muted print of red cabbage roses and green leaves. She wondered then if Kevin shared the same interest in Sheila that she seemed to have for him. In watching them together she thought that at least they complemented each other in appearance—she with her chic way of dressing and animated speech and he, tall and massive, dressed impeccably in a dark gray suit and blue shirt and blue print tie.

She stood watching them for a few more minutes, feeling suddenly left out. Nice party in my honor, she thought, when no one knows I'm even here. It was then that Kevin's eyes left the vivacious Sheila and rested on her, realizing full well that she had been staring at them.

She couldn't help the abrupt little start she gave as his eyes met hers, but she tried to cover it by turning quickly and she knew, ungracefully, in the direction of the tables set up with all the food delicacies.

She realized that his gaze had followed her as she walked, and when she reached the tables, she deliberately left her back turned toward him and started to pile a little of each hors d'oeuvre on a huge plate. She noted that all of the food—from fluffy miniature potato cakes, stuffed mushrooms, cubes of wicklow pancake, to Hafners sausages and Dublin coddle, though pleasing to the eye and delectable to the nostril was doing nothing to entice her appetite. It was all Kevin Sanford's fault, she thought. Her mood, her lack of appetite, her decision to leave Dublin—everything was Kevin's fault. No, she thought. No, no. It couldn't be happening to her. Yet, what else could it be. Even while he was berating her, telling her over and over that she should leave Merrion Square, she had felt the churning within her and the clamminess of her hands. And now, though he remained at the far end of the room, just the awareness of his presence was making her tremble. Did he know? She doubted it, and she wouldn't let him know, either. Never. She wouldn't weaken to that obstinate man with the dark moody

69

eyes and sensitive face. Sheila—she would rely on Sheila with her provocative gestures and elegant sophisticated clothes to keep his mind from realizing these childish emotions that had stirred in her. They had to be childish. After all, he hated her. How could she possibly have these feelings for a man who totally despised her? She was lost, lonely, and discouraged and even homesick to boot. But the stirrings were there. They had been there from the beginning when he had first barged into her room without knocking. But he would never know about them if she could help it. He would hate her more if he did. Hadn't she hurt him deeply by mentioning his wife's name to him that morning? It had been a cruel thing to do, yet he had been cruel to her. She had thought that one of the reasons he disliked her might be his resentment of her filling in for the deceased Nora by passing time with Moira. She had wanted to bring out that possibility—speak about it right in the open—to dispel his fears that she might be attempting this on purpose. But she had blown the whole discussion. "Welcome to Merrion Square, Greg Connors's daughter," was all he had answered. Perhaps if she knew more about Greg Connors, her own father, she would know what he had meant.

She put her plate down then, filled to the brim with everything she had taken in order to pass the time away. Wasteful, she thought. She would leave it all on the table, untouched, for someone else to savor. As she turned, Kevin was still watching her, his eyes completely clearing Sheila's head. As she looked over to him, his lips broke into a slow smile, as if he knew that she had spent time at the table to get away from

"You sound as though you're very familiar with Ireland."

He laughed. "I've been here a few times on business. I'm with a public relations firm in New York. My job is to search out biographies of men who are about to make it, so to speak, in different walks of life. Many times their backgrounds go back to the British Isles or Europe. I find out how they spent their summers as children, or who their aunts and uncles were . . . you know, anything to make them look good to their public or board of directors."

"That sounds like extremely interesting work."

"Well, it takes me to some interesting spots. Sometimes I even meet some interesting people . . . like this minute for instance," he said, giving her a disarming smile.

"Well, I appreciate the compliment," she blushed.

"Of course, I'm very efficient in my work. Usually get most of the assignment over within a day, giving myself a few extra days to enjoy my surroundings."

"Isn't that cheating a bit on your boss?" she laughed.

"Not really. I always have a few odds and ends to check out. It's knowing how one works best . . . and that's how I work best. My work is always above expectation. I told you, I'm very efficient."

"How do you know Padrig, Brad?" she asked, half wondering aloud how a doer as this man described himself could come to be an acquaintance of the always dreaming Padrig Corot.

"I don't know Padrig," he chuckled.

"Oh, but I thought . . ."

"I ran into a friend of his whom I originally met a

few nights ago in one of the pubs in the Center. He said Padrig was having a bash for a very attractive American cousin. He suggested I come over with him. In other words, fair lady, I'm a gate crasher. Think your cousin will mind?"

"Padrig? No, I imagine not. Padrig loves parties with many in attendance. Of course, I can't answer for him. You might get thrown out on your ear yet. As a matter of fact, he's walking over right now, so you'll soon know."

Speaking of Padrig did seem to summon him from an obscure corner of the party and they both turned to watch his approach, his face bright with a wide grin.

"There you are, cousin. Hope you're having a bit of fun. This is all for you, you know," he said as he gave her an exaggerated hug. Before she could say anything, he had his hand extended to Bradford Ainsley. "I'm Padrig Corot," he continued. "The man who is fortunate enough to be this lovely lady's cousin."

"Bradford Ainsley here," Brad said, extending his own hand. "Yes, Terrace has told me how hospitable you've been to her since her arrival," he continued in smooth public-relations fashion while Padrig's eyelids fluttered in childish disbelief. "By the way, I hope you don't mind that I've crashed. I met up with your friend John O'Brien a few nights ago at Bailey's pub. We spent the whole evening together. Then I ran into him again this morning and he suggested that I come along here with him."

"Oh, John, one of the best. Don't be silly, I'm delighted that you've come. It's nice for my little cousin to talk to someone from the States. By the way, Terrace, have you seen Kevin at all?"

mind. The thought occurs to me now that I forgot to ask your permission."

"Are you going with that chap I saw you talking to in the garden?" he said, his voice tightening.

"One of them," she snapped and now looked at him full face.

"Who is he, one of Padrig's unsavory cronies?" Now it was his turn to snap.

"Why are you interested even if he were?" she answered tauntingly.

"Have a pleasant time then, Terrace Connors," he said snidely, as if patronizing a teen-ager about to go on her first date. As he brushed past her and continued up the steps, his shoulder pushed roughly against hers and she bit down heavily on her lip trying to contain a barrage of nasty comments that were about to flow in his direction. And yet, as angry as she was over his briskness, she felt a quivering at the pit of her stomach. The stirrings, she thought. The same prickling of her skin and sinking feeling within her every time he was near.

She tossed her head in defiance of her own suspicions of her emotions and continued down the stairs only to run headlong into Pegeen Corot.

"I . . . I'm sorry, Pegeen. I didn't see you," she said, noticing that the woman was bedecked in a fine dark-brown silk suit set off by a large topaz and pearl brooch.

"And where do you think you're going, may I ask," the woman said, noticing the trench coat she had donned before she left her room.

"I'm . . . going out to dinner. I won't be late."

"Well, I'm happy we went to all this trouble to give

77

you a party only to have you leave in the middle of it," her aunt smoldered.

She stared blankly at the woman and made doubly sure that her voice was controlled before she answered. "Pegeen, for a party that was given in my honor, I don't think anyone knew I was here. And if they didn't know I was here—I doubt that they'll notice that I've stepped out."

The woman stared at her resentfully. "I'd expect that from you, Terrace. Being your mother's daughter."

"Expect what?"

"Impudence."

"Well, if I'm impudent like my mother, then perhaps we both had a good reason. And what does my mother have to do with all this?"

"Your father should have married his own kind."

"I imagine you and he had a lot in common then," she said, and immediately knew that she had chalked up one more enemy in the family.

Pegeen bristled and turned toward the study without answering further.

It was not difficult to locate Bradford Ainsley in the crowd once she had descended the rest of the stairway. He was sitting on a chair very close to the fireplace in the larger reception room. And although the great number of standing guests almost hid him from view, his glowing hair and the attractive boyishness of his features were difficult to keep obscured.

He rose as soon as he saw her approaching him.

"Are we set? You look flustered. Being given a hard time about leaving the party?" he asked as his eyes followed Pegeen walking away from their direction.

"Not really. Let's go, Brad," she said, a bit on the desperate side.

"We'll walk. It's not too far from here." As they left the house and they alighted on the sidewalk, he took her hand in his and they strolled in the direction of the Center taking practically the same route as she had that morning.

"This was such a wonderful idea, Brad. Padrig was . . . very kind to have a party for me, but frankly it's good to get away."

"Is this your first visit to this part of your family, Terrace?"

"Yes, how did you guess," she laughed.

"I don't know. Just had a feeling about it, I guess." Again she had the feeling that she wanted to blurt out the whole nonsense of the trip. It was probably because he was from home that she wanted to confide in him. Well, not exactly San Francisco home. Her own home bordered on the Pacific Ocean and his on the Atlantic, but at least they were from the same continent. At the moment that was close enough to his being from home.

"A penny for your thoughts, love," he said, squeezing her hand and obviously noticing her silence.

"Oh, it's nothing, Brad. It's been a long day, nothing more."

"What made you take this trip at this time ? I mean, have you ever been curious about this side of the family before?"

"Yes, of course I was curious, but you see I've been at school—the School of Interior Design in San Francisco."

"I see. Deciding to furnish a few castles here in Ireland and meet the family to boot?"

"No, the trip has nothing to do with interior decorating. Although in the long run I'll probably get some ideas from it. The tale is really uninteresting, Brad," she hesitated.

"Try me, baby. I'm a good listener," he prompted. "You can tell me over dinner," he continued as he indicated the stone façade of a pub which was situated on O'Connell Street just a stone's throw from O'Connell Bridge.

He held the heavy, carved door for her as they both stepped into a smoke-filled interior which was dimly lit.

"They say that there are over a thousand pubs in Dublin and I think out of all of them, this is surely the best. We'll go in the back to the dining room," he said and took her hand to lead her through the bar area.

His grasp was firm against her fingers and she reaffirmed her original feelings that she was pleased he had asked her out to dinner. Brad seemed pleasant, easy to be with and uncomplicated.

"How about this table?" Brad asked.

"That would be fine," she answered.

Soon they were drinking huge larders of stout and being served steaming plates of steak and kidney pie which he had insisted on ordering for her.

"Are you sorry you left the party?" he asked between bites of dinner.

"No, of course not. You're like a breath of fresh air," she answered and then flushed as she realized what she had said.

"Been that bad, hmmm? The house seems very comfortable though. It couldn't be too unpleasant."

"No, it really hasn't been, Brad. I . . . well, I just think the timing of the trip was bad—for me and perhaps for the people at Merrion Square."

"I told you before, I'm a good listener."

"As I said, it's really nothing. Actually, it's all Aunt Agatha's doing."

"I see. That explains it all," he chuckled. "Now, just off the record, who is Aunt Agatha?"

"She's my maternal aunt. I've lived with her in San Francisco most of my life, ever since my parents died in a car accident. Anyway, it seems that Aunt Agatha had been saving for quite a while to send me on this trip."

"I see it all now. You've always wanted to meet the other side of the family and Aunt Agatha finally was able to grant your wish."

"No. I hardly knew of their existence actually."

"There you go. I was always able to sum up a situation accurately," he laughed.

"Oh, Brad."

"Well, I thought my story sounded pretty logical."

"Maybe that's it. Life isn't logical enough and that's what makes it so complicated. I really don't know why Aunt Agatha chose Ireland as the destination for my holiday. Aunt Ag wasn't very close to my father's side of the family. I don't think the people at Merrion Square were too pleased when my father married a homespun girl whose great-grandmother went west in a covered wagon. I guess Aunt Ag felt guilty that she didn't force herself to keep up correspondence for my sake at least. Still, this is the place she chose for my vacation. And since I didn't want to disappoint her, this is where I ventured. I don't think it was very practical of Aunt Ag to send me. That's why I agreed to make the trip."

"Because it wasn't practical," he said as a statement rather than a question.

"That's right. You see, Aunt Agatha . . . well, you should know Aunt Agatha."

"I'm not sure I really want to know Aunt Agatha if she's as dictatorial as you suggest."

"Aunt Agatha," she continued, disregarding his remark, "is a very practical lady. She's also raised me to be very practical. If she went through this much trouble to surprise me with a vacation to Ireland, it must be pretty important to her. I had to go along with it, Brad. It's the only thing she's ever . . ."

"Say it . . . coerced?"

"Okay . . . coerced me to do in my entire life," she sighed, realizing that she was definitely not going to mention that Aunt Agatha hoped she would meet someone interesting on the trip.

"I must give ol' Aunt Ag credit for one thing at least."

"And that is?"

"If she didn't force this vacation on you, we never would have met. Now that would have been very serious indeed, even more so than having a meddling old aunt."

"You're very flattering, Brad, but Aunt Ag is not a meddling aunt. She is very dear to me."

"I was just joking, love. You are a serious one after all. But tell me about the people at Merrion Square.

After all, a party-crasher should know something about the people he just visited," he laughed.

"They're all very nice, really. Yet, they are all involved in their own lives, and as I said, my arrival may not have occurred at a good time for them. Anyway, I don't think I'll be staying in Ireland very long."

"Don't think like that, I just met you. Padrig seems to be an amiable sort of guy."

"Oh, he's . . . quite a character. Yes, he is very sociable," she answered, not about to go into her cousin's problems of the heart and purse.

"And what about that other chap . . . Kevin . . . is it Kevin Sanford?"

"Yes, that's his name," she said, trying to control a hint of claret that she felt appearing in her cheeks. "He's not really a blood relative of mine. He was married to a distant cousin, but she had a fatal accident and he merely continued living at the house."

"What does he do? I mean what line of work is he into?"

"I'm not sure really. Padrig mentioned a few times that he had some trouble in business. But what that was and what he does now is not quite clear to me."

"They seem like an interesting group of people," he smiled.

"Yes, they are," she said aloud. You should know how interesting, she added silently to herself. "Actually, I'm very lucky to have been given this trip."

"Ah, luck is what this land is all about. If you're superstitious, Ireland is the place to be . . . with all the wee people, the pot of gold . . . and all that."

"Oh, I think that's merely what is written in children's stories," she laughed.

"No, not at all. This country is filled with legends of that sort and the stories are told in abundance by adults to other adults."

"Okay, I believe you. I guess I need brushing up on the other half of my heritage."

"Yes, that, and you need to get in some sightseeing and begin acting like a real tourist. What would ol' Aunt Ag say if she learned you've merely taken a quick jaunt around the Center. I'll tell you what. Let's skip coffee and I'll take you on your first guided tour. There's no one better to guide you through Dublin than a full-fledged native New Yorker," he laughed as he beckoned the waiter to give him the dinner check.

She watched him as he paid the check and rose to help her out of her seat. She couldn't help feeling that the last few hours had been the most relaxed she had spent since her arrival in Dublin. He was very easy going, extremely smooth, and very polished. Most of all, he made her feel at ease. Aunt Ag would be pleased at her feeling relaxed with someone like Bradford Ainsley. But one thing she was sure that Aunt Agatha would disapprove of and that was through all of her good feelings and pleasure over being out with Bradford Ainsley, Kevin's brooding, sensitive face kept passing through her mind.

Chapter 7

The night air was crisp, yet the slow breeze held promise of warmer nights not too far off. The sidewalk in front of the pub was bustling with people coming and going to other hotels and night spots that were in the area.

Brad took her hand and led her down the sidewalk that ran parallel to the Liffey, and the glitter of the city, which had suddenly dressed in lights of all variances, startled her as she gasped at its beauty.

"You're impressed," he laughed. "It's a little like Christmas."

"It's a lovely night, Brad," she said, not bothering to hide her exuberance. "The air, the city lights . . . everything seems to hold a promise of . . ."

"A promise of excitement," he finished for her.

"Yes," she smiled. "I do sound like a tourist, don't I?"

"That's quite all right," he said, squeezing her hand. "Don't apologize, Terrace. Don't be afraid to feel."

She knew he was looking down at her, his towering height in obvious contrast to her five foot four frame. How close he had come in his comment to the saddest part of her life. She had never cared deeply or felt anything strongly. Was this a result of trying to fit into a household that was not her own since early childhood—feeling so grateful that Agatha Warren had

Moira, wondering if Moira were able to speak, would she become the only member of the family there who would befriend her. It was strange how her visit to this house rekindled all the feelings of loneliness that Aunt Agatha spent so much time trying to obliterate in her own way and which she, Terrace Connors, had felt were no longer prominent within her.

Then her mind switched to conjure the image of Kevin, with his tousled hair and accusing eyes. How could he infuriate her so much, and yet at the same time place her emotions in such a turmoil? And suddenly she smiled, and she knew why for so long a time she felt she could not feel any deep emotion. How could anything penetrate the accumulation of the one emotion that she had suppressed within her? In looking back, she could not remember having fully reacted to the knowledge that her parents were gone, never to return to her, never to be seen again. She remembered quite distinctly the afternoon that Agatha had sat her down next to her in the small parlor of the house, and it was a parlor, with all the Victorian fixtures that went with such a title for the room.

"Terrace," her aunt had said, "I'm going to tell you something that you must be very brave over. I would want you to be brave, child, as I don't know if I could cope if you took this any other way."

And then she was told about the tragedy. And when she was told, she remembered something clicking inside of her. Aunt Agatha was the only one she had left to take care of her. And Aunt Ag said that she wouldn't be able to cope unless she were brave. And she wouldn't want to upset Aunt Ag—since she loved Aunt Ag. Besides, Aunt Ag was the only one left to take care of her. Then she remembered that Agatha had hugged her very hard, and she had hugged her back. Yet she hadn't shed any tears. No, she had to be brave.

"Oh, poor Aunt Agatha," she blurted out now to the blank wall in front of her. "Oh, Aunt Ag, I missed them so much," and now her words were mixed with sobs that became more apparent as tears welled over the brim of her eyes and came streaming down her face. These tears were different from those she had shed as a child over a scraped knee or a broken bike. These were the tears that were suppressed for years, and she cried them out with a fervor and urgency that she had never known she possessed.

"And now," she said aloud, as she was wiping her face with a tissue, "to get on with the rest of my life."

As she prepared for bed, she thought of Brad again, and his plea for her to stay longer in Ireland. And then she realized that although her emotions had been bottled up for so many years and she was afraid to feel, there was another reason why she had pulled away from Brad in the park. Yes, part of it was being fearful, and yet the other part was being quite honest with herself. She would like to see Brad again, but he would not be the one that would stir her completely. And as her mind went to Kevin Sanford, she decided to go to sleep and let the future unfold itself spontaneously.

Chapter 8

Sun came streaming through the diningroom windows, and although her sleep had been troubled the night before, Terrace felt refreshed and somewhat invigorated.

Sheila was at the buffet table pouring herself a cup of coffee. She was eyeing the ham rasher and pudding that were displayed near the plate of fluffy scrambled eggs. Terrace felt disappointed that she would have to eat her breakfast with the other girl. Still, she was thankful that Kevin was not in sight, and decided to make the best of it.

"Good morning," she said as cheerfully as possible. She stood beside Sheila pouring her own coffee.

"Well, Terrace," the other girl hesitated as she looked her over. "What an attractive frock."

"In other words, Sheila, a bit too lightweight for May in Dublin."

"Nonsense. You shouldn't be so on the defensive. It's quite a lovely print. Come, Terrace, get your breakfast and sit with me," Sheila cooed as she found a place at the table.

Terrace took a deep quiet sigh, filled her plate with rashers and black and white pudding and then topped it all with a heaping amount of the fluffy eggs. Nerves, she thought. Nerves, insecurity, and loneliness were inciting her to eat like a bandit in flight.

"Now, let's talk," Sheila said as soon as she settled herself at the table.

"What about, Sheila? I mean, what possible thing do we have to talk about?" Her tone of voice was not as piercing as the words themselves. Actually, she felt in a fairly light mood and decided to go along with Sheila.

"You mustn't have bad feelings toward me, Terrace. Actually, Kevin and I are very pleased at your new interest. He's quite attractive. Kevin is delighted that you've found someone to . . . to occupy your time."

"Kevin said that?"

"Well, of course. He's not a close relative of yours, dear, but he still maintains a sense of family. He's always been like that. Even Nora's death hasn't changed that in him."

"How long . . . was he married to Nora before the accident?" she ventured.

"Just a year. Kevin . . . well, Kevin has come through a lot of things with a great show of strength. But everything bad is over now. He'll have nothing but happiness ahead of him. I'm going to see to that," she said defiantly.

"I imagine what Nora's death must have done to him."

"Yes, it was upsetting. He almost didn't marry her at all. He shouldn't have, you know. But there was always a sense of family there—a sense of responsibility," she sighed.

"Why did he almost not marry her, Sheila?" she asked, knowing that she should curtail her interest.

"I thought you knew the story," Sheila answered lazily as she lit a cigarette.

"Sheila, I know very little about the family. I know very little about my own parents. I thought I'd get some insight into my background while visiting here, but . . . well, none of you have been very communicative."

"Poor Terrace," Sheila drawled as she leaned back in her chair to study Sheila. "Darling, I'd be happy to tell you just about anything you want to know. Of course, I didn't know your parents. I'm just a year or two older than you are."

"I didn't know you realized that," Terrace smiled.

"Now, Terrace. We should be friends. After all, when I marry Kevin, I'll be . . . well, a sort of cousin. I mean Kevin is your cousin, isn't he?"

"No."

"Well, of course, he is!"

"Kevin is not related to me at all," she answered quietly between bites of ham. "Kevin married a distant cousin of mine. Only through marriage does he have any connection with me at all."

"Oh? I must say, Terrace, for someone who knows nothing about her family background—you certainly have that straight in your mind."

"Yes, haven't I? Now, what were you saying about Kevin and Nora?"

Sheila eyed her sullenly, then shrugged her shoulders and went on. "Kevin's family was very close to Nora's father. Her mother had died when Nora was in her early teens. When Nora's father was dying a few years later, he told Kevin that he was not worried about Nora's future. He was sure Kevin would look after her. Kevin and Nora had grown up together."

"And so he married her?"

"Supposedly, he was very torn. He respected Nora and was very fond of her. But he didn't love her."

"Really, Sheila?" Terrace said curtly.

"No, everyone knew it, Terrace. Everyone but Nora. She was too saddened by her father's death and too consoled by Kevin to see the true picture. Once he married her, he never let it be said that he didn't care for her. He was attentive, companionable . . . well, an excellent husband. They had a good year together," she said a bit wistfully.

"And now she's gone."

"Yes."

"And you're ready to take her place?"

"No, never. Ours will be a different relationship. Filled with excitement and love."

"I see," she said. "And when is this wedding to take place?"

Sheila hesitated. "Soon. Very soon. He's expecting some money, you see . . . a legacy. We'll live permanently in Paris. I think Kevin would like that. Life would be interesting for him then. He's had some business problems. But he'd like living in Paris," she said, her eyes shining from some mystical scene that only she could see.

"What kind of business problems did he have, Sheila?"

Sheila looked at Terrace blankly, as if awakened from private sleep. "I'm not sure exactly. He was in banking while he was married to Nora. Then suddenly, he was writing. He became very conservative with his expenditures. Although when he was married to Nora she never lacked for anything," she answered.

Terrace smiled at Sheila. "Had it ever occurred to

101

you, Sheila, that he may just have wanted to write? Perhaps material things are not important to him."

"Nonsense. I'm sure he'll give up all of this writing business once we marry. I'm trying to persuade him to go back to banking. It's much more fruitful."

"Yes, and then you'll have a steady amount of his money to spend," laughed Terrace.

"I think you've missed the point. Anyway I must go. I have work to do. I think Kevin is proud that I'm in fashion work. He is drawn to interesting and exciting people," she said as she drew herself up from the table and left the room abruptly and without another word.

Terrace stared after the girl incredulously. If she stayed the summer, she thought, she might eventually learn all about the people there and perhaps even something about her own parents. But, would it be worth it? No, she would leave at the end of the week. Her parents were gone and she lamented the relationship that they never had together. Yet, there was no way to regain that now, and nothing she could learn about them could bring them back.

Then she thought of the other people in the house. There was nothing that she wanted from any of them—except . . . Kevin? Kevin, with his brooding and searching eyes and deep, sensitive face. Did she want something from him? If she lingered at Merrion Square any longer than a week more, she knew what the answer would be. He had stirred her somehow. And even his curt and pungent remarks could not take away the sensation that filled her being when he was close by. A schoolgirl's physical infatuation—perhaps. Yet the stirrings that he caused in her were far from a youngster's feelings, and these were becoming so strong in her that even Brad's attention to her became secondary in importance.

The sun continued to pour through the windows and now it touched her face and warmed her as she sat back in her chair and closed her eyes to let it caress her totally. She had come to Dublin with nothing and she would leave the same way. And yet, if she did not leave soon, she would carry with her a deep regret that she and Kevin never came to know each other better. He had been abrupt and almost resentful of her presence there. But was all that really directed toward her? Couldn't it all be a result of the series of bad experiences he had been through? He had taken a very large step in marrying Nora out of pity for her circumstances. Then she was killed only a year after their marriage.

She opened her eyes then and squinted away the sunlight that was still lingering across her face. She wouldn't dote on it any longer. She wouldn't dote on the family and especially on Kevin. The day was bright and she would do something for Moira that morning and perhaps some positive activity around the house would rub off on the others.

She found Lizbeth just as she was coming down the staircase.

"Good morning, Miss Connors. It's such a beautiful day. We'll be getting more of these as the month goes along."

"Yes, I was just seeking you out for that very reason. Is Padrig about, Lizbeth?"

"No, miss. He's gone to the Center. Left early this morning, he did."

"Oh, that's too bad," she answered.

"Well, is it something that I might help you with, then?"

"No, I wanted Padrig to help carry something . . ." she hesitated.

"Well, there's Mr. Sanford, miss. He's about the house. I think he's up on the top floor. Said he would be doing some research. What was it that needs carrying, miss? I'm pretty strong myself."

"I know you are, Lizbeth. And also, may I add that you've been very helpful to me since I've arrived. I want to thank you for that."

"Oh, think nothing of it. I know that Miss Moira's life will be brighter now that you're here."

"Actually, it was Moira whom I was thinking of when I asked for Padrig. Wouldn't it be a grand idea to bundle her with blankets and have her sit outside in the sun for a while."

"Oh, miss, that would be a wonderful idea. With the cold weather and dampness until now, this would be her first outing."

"I don't think we'll be able to manage it, Lizbeth—not without help."

"But, I am very strong, Miss Connors."

"I realize that, but we'll have to carry Moira in a position comfortable to her. We couldn't have any mishaps."

"Yes, you're right, there. Suppose I go up and ask Mr. Sanford to give us a hand, then. I'm sure he'll oblige us."

"You said he was on the top floor?"

"Yes, miss. I don't know what he's searching for. Those rooms haven't been used in years. Most of them contain a lot of excess furniture that is no longer used by the family."

"Lizbeth, why don't you go and prepare Moira for the outing. I'll get a sweater and go up and ask Mr. Sanford if he would help us."

"Oh, that's a fine idea," Lizbeth said as she picked up her skirts and disappeared up the staircase.

Terrace lingered awhile holding on to the bannister and wondering if Kevin Sanford would mind the intrusion. She knew that he did not like the idea of her attending to Moira. Was it painful for him to see someone taking Nora's place? Well, there was no other way, she thought. Moira should be out in the sun having a break from the confinement of her room. There was no way to tell how long Padrig would be away from the house, and she and Lizbeth could not handle Moira alone. It had to be Kevin, then, who would have to help them. Sooner or later he had to realize that life had to go on.

She had never been on the top floor of the house before, and though there was not a spot of dust to be seen, the atmosphere was of mustiness. The corridor was mostly darkened as the closed doors of the rooms cut off any rays of sun that might have added life to the area.

She did notice a small ray of light at the far end of the hall though, and surmised that this is where Kevin was working. She softened her footsteps as she approached the room and found that the door was half opened. She saw a small study with bookshelves lining the walls and a large mahogany desk gracing its center. The walls were wood paneled and a dark green carpet covered the floor.

Kevin Sanford had not noticed her arrival as he busied himself pulling out large volumes from the bookshelves, leafing through them quickly and placing them at random on top of the desk. Once again she had the opportunity to watch him without being noticed or without wanting to run away from his gaze. As she viewed him now, she realized that he was quite a bit older than she, probably in his late thirties. He was squarely built and tall, without being exceedingly so. Now, as she watched him, his brow was furrowed, as if he were fighting some inner turmoil of his own.

She stepped back a few paces from the door and then made sure that her feet scuffed the floorboards before she reentered the doorway. He was leaning over the desk, but his eyes shot up immediately, his brow still furrowed and his eyes troubled and dim. He stared at her a few seconds as if she were a stranger to the world that he had created for himself in that room. She did not utter a word as she looked at him and soon she saw his features relax as he came back to the present. She thought he was about to smile, but he caught himself as his face colored slightly and he merely straightened from his position over the desk.

"What is it, Terrace Connors? What brings you up here seeking me out?"

"I . . . wonder if you could do me a favor?" she said, barely hearing her own voice at all.

"A favor? My, I would think that I'd be the last person you would ask for something like that," he answered and she knew he was mocking her.

"Well, Padrig is in town and . . ."

"I see. I was right then. I am the last person around and you have no other choice."

"That's about right," she said, clenching her teeth. She wondered how a man who infuriated her so could also create the stirrings that formed at the pit of her stomach—those same stirrings which were responsible for her breath coming out in rushes.

"Well, what is this chore that is so important you had to come to me instead of waiting for Padrig?" His face was in a sly expression now and she knew he was purposefully playing on her patience.

She looked at him without speaking, her eyes narrowed to slits to keep out the fury that blazed through them. She almost felt like canceling the outing for Moira, but then had second thoughts on the matter.

"It's such a warm and lovely day that I'm taking Moira out to sit in the garden. Lizbeth and I don't feel that we could manage transporting her. I thought . . . well, do you think you could help us?"

He looked at her blankly and then his face broke into one of his rare but attractive broad smiles.

"What's the matter?" she asked as she felt herself flushing.

He looked down at the desk and pretended to straighten a few of the volumes there, all the while fighting the amusement that seemed to want to cross his face.

"Well?" she asked again, showing her impatience.

He looked up at her, his face sobered, and then he said, "You, Terrace Connors. It's beginning to seem that you're the matter."

She froze, not knowing what he meant, and very definitely afraid that she was about to read the wrong meaning into his vague statement.

"Are you going to help me, Kevin Sanford?" she

asked, both her hands on her hips, now trying to show annoyance to cover her exasperation.

"Of course, of course. How could I refuse you? It will probably be the only time you'll ever ask me to do something for you," he said, going back easily to his saucy airs.

"Will you come now?"

"Yes, yes," he laughed. "I would never keep you waiting," and he made a swooping gesture indicating that she should lead the way.

He was laughing at her, she thought—laughing at her just as Sheila had. She hated him and yet as she felt his presence following her down the staircase, she realized that there was something stronger than hate that she felt for this man—and she didn't know what to do about it. Whatever it was, she could not let it run rampant. And more than anything, he must not know that she had these feelings. They would laugh harder if they knew, both he and Sheila. He liked sophisticated women . . . like Sheila . . . and everything exciting, like Paris . . . and women with interesting careers. Sheila said he did. Sheila said that they would marry.

It was easily understood why he ran into her at the bottom of the steps. She had stopped cold to think of him and Sheila, stopped dead in her tracks to think of him in Sheila's Paris apartment. And he, following very closely behind her, had now run directly into her.

"What's wrong?" he asked as she automatically turned to face him. "Why did you stop?" he continued—and then it happened.

He was looking down at her, his expression at first perplexed over the reason she had paused in her tracks. And then his face relaxed as she told him silently, without a word spoken. She told him with her eyes, and with her lips that said nothing but which were parted slightly now as she looked at the disarray of his wavy hair and the sensitivity of his mouth. And he seemed to hear it all as his eyes widened at first with surprise and then merely twinkled with a definite merriment of recognition.

Terrace Connors, you have lost all semblance of pride, she thought. He knows. You told him by the way you looked at him, by the way you longed for him to be closer and let it show in your eyes . . . closer than the distance he was now from you. He knows that you want him to touch you, to hold you. Cover, Terrace Connors. Cover before it's too late.

"I was just thinking . . . do we need anything from the top floor that could serve as a conveyance to get her to the garden?" Her voice was beautiful—cool and detached. His brow furrowed again. He was thinking that she was playing games with him. Let him think anything but the truth. Perhaps she would leave Dublin earlier than a week . . . leave him to his mourning, to his resentfulness of how life had treated him . . . without being there with him to try to soothe him . . . to try to make him see that he had his whole life ahead of him.

His face was serious as he spoke. It was over. The moment had passed. He could never be sure that he had read her correctly those few moments before.

"I don't think we need anything but her chaise," he said as he now passed her and was entering Moira's bedroom ahead of her.

"Lizbeth, have you wrapped her well?" he asked as

109

he leaned over, and to Terrace's amazement, kissed Moira gently on her forehead and scooped her in one movement from the bed to the chaise.

· "Oh yes, Mr. Sanford. You know how well I take care of the mistress."

"Yes, indeed, I do," he said quietly. "All right, this shouldn't be as big a chore as Miss Connors is making it out to be. Lizbeth, you and Miss Connors hold the foot end of the chaise. I'll take the back end which is the heaviest. One on each side now. All right, lift."

They followed his initial direction and then proceeded in silence down the staircase one step at a time. Once or twice he reminded them to keep their end of the chaise high enough so that Moira would not slip forward. The older woman seemed undisturbed at the activity, and once Terrace thought there was a look of pleasure on her face at the attention being given her. It was only after the staircase had been conquered that Kevin spoke at any length, and this was between intakes of air from the energy that had been exerted on the steps.

"You see . . . nothing at all to it . . . surprised you didn't get your friend . . . what is the chap's name . . . Ainsley . . . to help you with a simple activity like this. Or, is he gone from Dublin?"

Terrace looked back over her shoulder and felt his eyes staring through her. "No, he's still here. As a matter of fact, he's taking me to lunch," she answered, as they continued transporting Moira through the long hallway toward the garden door.

"What does he do, this Ainsley?"

"He's in public relations," she said over her shoulder.

"For whom?"

"I don't know. It wasn't important to me, and I don't see why it should be to you," she snapped.

There was silence for a few minutes and then he directed them to place the chair under the two trees that were located on the far side of the garden.

"Is that all, Terrace Connors? I mean, am I needed for any more heavy work?"

"No, I think that will be it," she answered, without looking directly at him.

"I'll leave you now to get on with your amusement of Aunt Moira so that you'll not be late for your luncheon."

"Thank you. That's very considerate of you."

"Lizbeth. Is Sheila about?" he asked, turning his back to Terrace.

"No, Mr. Sanford. But she left word for you to wait for her and not to leave without her, sir."

"No, I had no intention of doing that," he said as if to himself, and then reentered the house.

Chapter 9

She stared sullenly at the door he had closed behind him as if accusing it of causing her disappointment. He was meeting Sheila. What else was she to expect? Sheila did say that they were to marry, and why would she make a statement of that sort if it were not true? It seemed foolish to dangle in front of him the fact that she was to have lunch with Bradford Ainsley. Did she think he would really care? He had his own life, which did not include her at all. Yet, somehow, Sheila was included. How deeply she was included was not important now. But she had all the advantages. She was attractive, vivacious, with stylish clothes and an interesting job. And she had known him for a long while. He had given up so much to comfort Nora only to become a widower after one year of marriage. Sheila would be good for him. She would lift him from the saddened life he had led until then.

"Miss Connors? Miss Connors, is there something wrong?" Lizbeth had her hand on Terrace's arm as she beckoned her away from her thoughts.

It was only then that she realized she was still staring at the door that led into the house, the door that Kevin had passed through to go to look for Sheila.

"No. No, Lizbeth, everything is fine." She turned away from the house with a defiant toss of her head and walked toward her invalid aunt. "Lizbeth, if it warms a little more, perhaps lunch could be served here in the garden."

"Oh, that would be a treat for your aunt, miss. But what about your luncheon appointment with Mr. Ainsley?"

"That's right. I'd forgotten about that." For a moment she felt that she wanted to cancel her plans with Brad. Uncomplicated, casual Brad. "Well, Lizbeth, we could serve Moira a little earlier than usual. I'll feed her out here in the garden and still be ready for Mr. Ainsley."

"That's fine, miss. Your aunt will appreciate that. I'll leave you with her then," she said as she entered the house.

Terrace sat in a garden chair near Moira. The woman's face was serene and her eyes looked directly at her niece.

"Aunt Moira," she said smiling down at her. "You must forgive my awkwardness. I'm not a very good angel of mercy. I know I won't be as entertaining or as accommodating as Nora was. Yet my willingness is strong. Are you comfortable, Moira? I wish I could know if you're comfortable."

The woman's eyes remained serene, blinking normally, still looking at her with a childlike gaze that touched her heart. She did notice that her hands seemed restless and although they were clasped, her index finger seemed to move at random.

"I know you're very curious about me, aunt, not having heard from Aunt Agatha or me all these years. It wasn't Agatha's fault though. She tried her best, you know. Why, she didn't know when Mother left me there to go on a trip with my father that it would be an arrangement for life. It came as a shock to her, the entire situation did."

Her aunt seemed to be taking in the conversation, listening intently, and yet her hands were still a bit restless.

"Of course, the accident hit her very hard. She was very close to both my parents. Then on top of that, there was me to care for, you see. She did the best she could. So, please don't be angry at the lack of communication from us. I think, well, I think Agatha felt that my mother was not . . . accepted too well here. And after being here, I think all that must have come from Pegeen.

"Now don't be upset by my saying that," she paused, and patted her aunt's still restless fingers. "I don't think we should have any secrets, and that's why I'm being frank with you. I want you to know the reasons why Aunt Ag didn't write."

She smoothed back her aunt's hair and looked around the garden. The early bloomers sent a potpourri of scent to her nostrils and she heaved a deep sigh. This outing would do her good as well as her invalid aunt, she thought.

"But I did have a good life growing up. Of course, Aunt Ag did not have much money, and what she had she shared with me."

Here, her aunt's hands were more restless than ever. Again she patted them, hoping to calm the woman.

"Now, you must try to relax, aunt. This is a good spot for your chaise. Your eyes are shaded against the sun, yet its rays are warming the rest of you. Don't you agree, Moira?"

Now she saw the woman's index finger rise and then fall back to her lap again.

"You are a bit restless, aunt. Would you rather have stayed in your room, I wonder."

Now she saw her aunt's finger go up and down twice. Suddenly, she was taken with an uncanny feeling.

"Aunt Moira," Terrace was breathless and wondered if she would do more harm in sharing her thoughts, or whether she should let them be until she was certain. Yet, how else could she be certain unless she asked. "Aunt Moira, are you trying to communicate with me by the movement of your index finger?"

Her aunt's finger went up quickly in just one movement.

"Does one movement mean yes, aunt, and two movements a negative answer?"

Again the finger went up just once.

"I don't want to tire you, Moira, and it's not that I don't believe you. But you must understand that it's important for me to know. Answer me with your finger, Moira. Is it snowing out?"

The finger moved twice.

"Is it raining out, Moira?"

Again there was double movement.

"Is it a lovely, sunny day?"

Now the finger moved once. The excitement that filled the girl was overwhelming and her skin prickled with emotion.

"Did Nora know you could do this, Moira? I mean did she know that you could communicate with your index finger?"

There was a long hesitancy before Moira moved her finger twice.

"She didn't know, then?"

Again there was a pause before the double movement.

"You're not quite sure how to answer."

The finger made one quick movement.

"Then I'll have to rephrase the question. Am I tiring you, Moira? I don't want to tire you."

There were two quick movements and then another quick two movements.

"You're anxious for this, then. Of course you would be. You're bursting to communicate," she said as she patted the woman's arm. In doing this, her eye caught the figure in the open second-floor window. It was Kevin, blatantly staring down at her with no effort to hide his stance. He must wonder, she thought, what possible topic could be occupying her conversation with her aunt. From his distance there would be no way for him to see Moira's finger movements. She resolved at that moment that she would tell no one of Moira's ability to communicate until she herself was sure that the method was almost foolproof. There would be no reason to raise the hopes of the family for something that she had merely contrived in her imagination. She looked up at the second-story window again and was relieved to see that Kevin was no longer there.

"Let's get back to . . . our conversation, Moira. Nora did not know you could communicate. But, was she working on this type of communication with you?"

Her aunt moved her finger just once.

"I wonder . . . Nora was supposedly into nursing. Was she into physical therapy?"

The answer was yes.

"Now I can see it all. Nora spent a lot of time with you trying to give you the ability to move your fingers. And once she had the accident, you continued on your own until you had their use."

Again her aunt answered yes.

"You knew what Nora was trying to accomplish and you continued every day, alone in your room, to use the muscles of your finger."

The finger gave an affirmative movement.

"Oh, Aunt Moirā. You were doing this by your own efforts—determined one day to communicate with the rest of the family. I am so proud of you, and at the same time I feel so badly that you had to go through it all on your own." With that she leaned over to embrace the woman and give her an affectionate kiss on the forehead.

As she lifted her head to look at her aunt, she noticed a sudden change came over the older woman. Her eyelids began to flutter quickly, almost uncontrollably. Then the eyes themselves filled with tears which began to stream down her face.

"All right, aunt. All right, be calm now. You're upset about something." The finger moved once and a sudden panic filled Terrace that she had started something that not only would be harmful to the woman but which she had no power to control.

"Yes, I know you're upset, aunt. Is it this communication that's doing it, Moira?"

The fingers moved twice as Terrace dried her aunt's tears with some tissue that Lizbeth had left nearby.

"It's not the communication. Then, it must be the frustration of it all. There's so much to tell, and this method is ever so slow. That must be it? No? Then . . . then there is one particular thing that you want to tell me, and I've not even approached the subject, and you cannot bring it up yourself? Yes, that's it," she cried, noticing the single movement of the finger.

She sat back in her chair, exhausted from the activity that she and the woman had just been through.

"Moira, rest a moment, and let me collect my thoughts. If I'm feeling this drained, you must indeed be exhausted as well." She looked straight into her aunt's eyes and knew from their brightness that Moira wanted no rest. Her eyes were shining with excitement as the woman realized that she and her niece were on the brink of important communication.

"I know, Moira. Now that we've begun, it's difficult to pause. Still, this degree of excitement is not good for you. And besides, my mind is going off in different directions. Close your eyes for a while. Let me catch up to myself," she said as she patted the woman's arm in a lulling motion.

Moira finally succumbed to her suggestion and was even dozing after a few minutes. Terrace leaned back in her chair and took a deep sigh of relief. For a moment, she thought she would never be able to comfort Moira. If she hadn't quieted as soon as she did, she would have been forced to summon Kevin. Oh, he would have been upset at Moira's unhappiness, and yet she knew there would be a gloat of an I-told-you-so expression on his face. He had warned her not to bother Moira. He had told her that Lizbeth was very capable of caring for her. But even though she would

118

have received the just due of his anger, he would have had to be summoned. Yes, she was certainly relieved that she did not have to summon Kevin, but most of all she was content that Moira had quieted.

They had been doing so well, she thought. The discovery that Moira could communicate at all was thrilling. And it should have been thrilling to the older woman also. Of course, her eyes had been bright with excitement at first. And yet the tears came. Something was upsetting the woman, and she was aghast to think that she may never be able to learn what that was. How could she really help Aunt Moira any longer since she had no frame of reference to the woman's life except for her most recent days.

The other members of the family would be able to work with Moira more quickly than she could, of course. They would know what her life was like before her accident and what could be pressing on her mind from that time that she so vehemently wanted to express now. Still, could she dare mention to the family that Moira was able to communicate? Was she that sure of the woman's new-found agility, or were the finger movements merely a coincidence to the questions she just happened to ask her? Perhaps this was the reason for the woman's tears. Perhaps she became frustrated to think that her niece assumed she could communicate when she could not.

There was no way that she could tell the family at this point. It would be a disaster to give them all hope when she wasn't certain. Yet the woman's answers with her finger had been so logical in respect to her questions. She would have to work with her again and very soon.

"There you are, my dear cousin," Padrig's voice came bellowing from the open door to the house, his eyes shining with some mischief that only he knew about.

"Hush, Padrig. Moira has just dropped off for a nap. You're not to waken her," she whispered harshly to her cousin.

"Indeed I won't, Terrace. I was just looking out to see to your comfort."

"My comfort or were you looking out for my activities?" she said as she eyed him slyly.

"Now, what a thing to say. It's hurting my feelings you are," he answered in a thick brogue which she hadn't heard him use for a while.

"You're the one, Padrig, that mentioned you were a rogue."

"But to you I'm nothing less than a gentleman, my dear cousin."

"Then if you are, Padrig, help me carry Moira's chaise back up to her room. I thought I would give her lunch out here, but I think she had enough for one day. Perhaps Kevin would help us."

"No, dear cousin. Kevin has gone to the Center with Sheila."

"It's not going too well for you, is it, Padrig?"

"I . . . well, if you're talking about Sheila, I guess it isn't. But let's get on with more serious matters of conversation. It looks as though you've gotten on well with dear Aunt Moira. Lizbeth claims you've been out here with her for most of the morning. It looks as though we've got ourselves a new favorite in the household—perhaps even a new heiress."

"Padrig!"

"Oh, now, I'm just kiddin' ye, cousin mine."

"You're beginning to sound just like Kevin."

"Oh, does he think you're here for motives other than seeing the sights?"

"I should say he does. From the first time he saw me he's been trying to decide what purpose of personal gain brought me here."

"Poor Terrace, being pulled in all directions for everyone's individual reasons."

"But your reasons were the most wasteful."

"Mine? I merely had a feeling we were all in a rut here. I thought it was time we had an outsider in our midst . . . keep our manners up with each other. You see how much joy you've given Moira. See how peacefully she's sleeping."

"Oh, Padrig, you're not to be believed. She takes a nap or even two every day. It surprises me that you think people actually swallow the weak excuses you give."

"Now, what do you mean by that?" he pouted.

"You know that my usefulness to you was to get Kevin away from Sheila."

"Well . . . that could have been an extra added nicety that might have come out of your visit. It still could come about, you know."

"I don't think there'll be time, Padrig. I'm only staying until the end of the week."

"Oh, you're not, now," he said, his expression actually looking disappointed. "Where have we gone wrong? Where have we offended you?"

"No one's offended me, Padrig. Then, again . . . I really don't think your mother is that pleased over having me here."

"I told you that in the beginning. She's only trying to make up for her own guilt. Never liked your mother, either."

"I gathered that."

"She was an outsider, too, like you are. She never thought your father should have married someone who was not from a prominent Dublin family."

"She wasn't close to my father either, then?"

"Not at all. It was Moira who doted on your father, and your mother as well. Moira would have taken you over here herself to care for you when your parents had the accident, but Pegeen would have made life miserable for you and she knew it."

"I'm surprised to hear you speak about Pegeen that way."

"Oh, yes. Well, even Padrig Corot must face the realities of life sometimes."

"Then why don't you try facing realities in directions other than your mother, Padrig?"

"Like . . . ?"

"Why don't you face reality in connection with Sheila?"

"I've been doing that now. I've been doing that."

"I'll bet you have," she said a bit snidely. "Anyway, Padrig, what you could do for me now is to help me carry Moira upstairs."

He answered by opening the door to the house and calling for Lizbeth who arrived almost in seconds to help carry the chaise and Moira up to her room. The woman stirred twice, but seemed in a deep sleep of exhaustion. In looking at her sleeping in the chaise, Terrace longed to tell the others of the communication that had taken place between them. And yet, she knew that she would have to work with Moira again before she told anyone of her discovery.

Moira had been made comfortable and Lizbeth had immediately shooed away Terrace and her cousin telling them to leave their aunt to her pleasant slumber.

It was on the landing that Padrig had taken her arm. "Terrace," he said, "you know I was serious when I said I was facing reality about Sheila."

She looked at him, stunned that he would bring up the subject again. "I'm sorry, Padrig. I guess I did cluck at you when you said that before. I should have heard you out," she said as she looked at her cousin and a wave of pity for him came over her.

"Don't apologize. It's my own fault that people don't take me seriously. But I've been doing a lot of thinking since we last spoke."

"Yes, Padrig?"

"Well, you know, you said I was good with the art of gab and telling stories of the old legends. You mentioned that I should try to develop something I was good at doing. And then I tried to think of another area that was interesting to me. And there it was, right in front of me, and I never realized it."

"And what is that, Padrig?" He seemed so excited and she hesitated to interrupt him.

"Now who do you think helped Lizbeth prepare all that food for the party yesterday?"

"I assumed it was Pegeen."

"Not at all," he said in a high brogue. "It was I, dear cousin. You see, I like to entertain. I like to prepare great feasts and have lots of people around."

"Padrig, what are you getting at?"

"Paddy Murphy's place out in the country is closing

down. It has been a country pub for many years, but the action is shifting to the city. You can see yourself how bustling Dublin is now. Well, anyway, Paddy's had two great chefs, Brian Meegan and—believe it or not—Gustav Penot, a citizen of France. Now these two will be out of work, so they're beginning to look for a place to demonstrate their culinary art."

"You mean that you would . . ."

"Yes, cousin, I think you've got the idea. I would love to open a little restaurant—a pub with a dining room serving food that would be fit for royalty. And you know what I'd call it, Terrace? I'd call it The Fairy Tree. Yes, I would," he said between her laughter. "And each menu would have a different legend written on it. And . . . and . . ."

"And, Padrig?"

"And all this chatter is for naught."

"But, why? I think all this is marvelous."

"Only one trouble, cousin. Brian and Gustav would be willing to work for me."

"Then there's no problem."

"Yes, there is. You see I don't have the cash to buy a place of my own."

"Oh, Padrig."

"I've squandered a lot in my life, I have. Never had direction to put it all into a specific undertaking. Then you sort of started me thinking. This Sheila thing—it wasn't real. You were right. I guess I was attaching myself to a free ride. Now this other, the pub . . . I'd really like to do it."

"I would like to see you do it, Padrig. I would like to see that very much."

"That's why you can't leave here so soon, Terrace.

You've helped. You've helped me a lot. You've made Moira happy and . . . well, we need you around here. Stay a little longer and help me figure this thing out, will you?"

She was touched that he was placing her in such a high position as to be the one who could straighten out the ills of the household. She hesitated, not wanting to shatter his newly found enthusiasm, and yet what could she answer him?

"Padrig, we'll talk more about this later. I . . . well, I think it's great. I'm sure there's something we could figure out. Let me dash now, Padrig. I'm supposed to meet Brad for lunch and I'm a little late."

"Okay," he said hopefully. "And Terrace?"

"Yes, Padrig?"

"I told you it was a good thing that you planned to visit us."

Chapter 10

Her copper hair glistened in the sun's rays as she ran the brush vigorously through its lengthy strands, while she seated herself at the vanity table. She had already freshened her makeup and now felt pangs of guilt as she allowed herself a few more minutes to tend to her coiffure while keeping Brad waiting. She realized that her guilt emanated half from the fact that she was very late, but mostly from her reluctance to see him at all. It had been a relief to talk to him in the garden at the reception, to hear the familiar American twang in his voice, and to escape from the various personalities in the house while he entertained her at one of the local pubs. His attention toward her in the park was even more elating and for a moment she felt wanted and sought after and she almost responded with more emotion than she thought she was capable of. And yet, she had stepped back and held him off. Because she was incapable of feeling? No. Because throughout the evening her attention kept leaving him and his conversation and focusing on the elusive and oversensitive Kevin Sanford.

Bradford Ainsley was a nice young man, uncomplicated, an easy talker, and comfortable. Had she seen him at a party in her own country, she would have commented to herself that he was a fairly attractive and nice person. Only here, in a foreign country, had he immediately become something special to her. And now, just a short time after their first meeting—when she had clutched onto him as the last straw in an otherwise cold abyss of strange personalities—she felt a peculiar reluctance at having to spend the next few hours with him.

Of course she was reluctant to leave the house, she thought. She should be spending the next few hours with Padrig, trying to help him untangle the predicament he was in; or taking time to work with Moira to learn once and for all the authenticity of her ability to communicate; or to wait patiently for Kevin to return from his appointment with Sheila when she could attempt to persuade him that she had not arrived in Dublin merely to gain something personally from the family.

"You've gotten yourself into a real mess, Terrace Connors," she told herself aloud in the mirror that faced her. "Somehow, in your short stay here, you've gotten yourself pretty involved with the family. What about touring Dublin Castle and Trinity College, Terrace Connors? What about the Book of Kells and all that other stuff that tourists are supposed to see? All that mean anything to you, Terrace Connors? Of course not. As a tourist, young lady, you fall very short of the mark," she snapped at herself.

She rose from the vanity and went to the closet to retrieve her brown jacket-sweater. As she was slipping it over her shoulders, her mind mused over Padrig. He said she had helped him reflect over Sheila Malloy and his future goals. Had she really been that helpful to him? It would please her if she had. And yet she really didn't mean to talk him out of trying for Sheila if he really cared for her. But Sheila had been beastly to him, throwing him not even small crumbs of sociability to say nothing of affection. She knew that Sheila cared nothing for Padrig, and in thinking further, she doubted that Padrig had any true feelings for her either. He had been merely grasping onto her shoulders to keep afloat in the future. This last fact is what she had aided him in realizing, if she had aided him at all.

And now she was ready to leave her room to meet Brad, who was probably pacing impatiently in the lower foyer. Was it really fair of her to see him at all since she felt nothing for him? Was his show of affection in the park something that she did not dare toy with at this time? Should she at least make a clean breast of it before they left the house—level with him that they could be friends, but nothing further could take place between them?

She was halfway down the stairs when she realized she had left her room at all. He was already there, as she had thought, pacing the front foyer.

"I'm sorry, Brad. I know I'm late . . . it . . . it just couldn't be helped."

"Not to worry, princess, I think I arrived a little on the early side anyway."

No, she couldn't do it. First of all, she didn't really know if he cared that much for her heart-to-heart chat to make a difference anyway. And if he did care . . . it would be too abrupt to merely stand there and make a statement to him without any preamble at all. The day would have to unfold spontaneously. That was the only way. At least she was happy that she didn't cancel the appointment altogether. He opened the door for her and they alighted on the sidewalk and began walking to the Center.

"Have you been working hard, Brad?"

"No, not more than usual," he answered.

He was sullen, she thought. Nonchalant and casual Brad was not supposed to be sullen. He was supposed to be chatty and casual and . . . of course she was being unfair. She had depended upon him in the beginning to be a leveling point against the affairs at Merrion Square. Then she had felt guilty—afraid she would be leading him on, this very nice and uncomplicated person. It was only now that she reminded herself that he was no puppet in his own right. He was alive and feeling, and now it seemed he was feeling sullen.

"I had a grand morning, Brad. I was out in the garden with Moira," she said, thinking that she would have to set a light mood for the afternoon.

"Moira was able to get down into the garden?" he asked as if merely trying without interest to keep up the topic of conversation.

"Oh, not on her own, unfortunately. We carried her down on her chaise. The weather has turned lovely."

"I wouldn't count on it staying this way. Like everything else in the world, baby, old Mother Nature is two-faced."

"Brad! That's not like you. Oh, I know what you're going to say. It's all part of your black-and-white practical philosophy of life. No illusions."

"That's . . . exactly it. As a matter of fact, that's what I want to talk to you about. Let's go in here. One pub is as good as another," he said as he took her arm and led her into a small pub situated just at the beginning of the commercial center.

"Two, please, for lunch," he said to the waiter who led them to a small paneled room to the rear of the bar.

As in the other pub he had taken her, the tables were set with white linen cloths, and at the center of each table stood a small carafe of mixed flowers.

"Brad, you always take me to places with such great atmosphere," she said, trying to calm his mood and pacify her own regret at having come on the outing at all.

"Yeh," he drawled. "It goes with the service."

They were seated by the waiter and without asking her first, Brad ordered two lagers and two orders of shepherd's pie.

"Brad? What's . . . is there something wrong?" she asked after the waiter had left them.

"Wrong? The world is wrong. You either go with that, or you get off. Now, in order to go with a wrong world, you must also be wrong. Contrary to the old adage that two wrongs don't make a right . . . in this case—to be wrong when the world is wrong means you'll make it. Do you understand, Terrace?" He was looking directly at her now, his eyes squinting as if he were trying to see the picture she was seeing through his words.

"No, Brad. I don't understand."

"You see, one has priorities. One person's priority is nothing to someone else. You have to take a stand, though, and come to terms with what is most important to you. That part's easy. It only gets tough if you come to the point when you want two things very badly at one time and the two things are impossible coming together like that."

The waiter brought their orders and when he left she asked, "What is it, Brad? I still don't understand you."

"I was thinking of the first time I saw you in the garden at the house on Merrion Square. Then I was thinking of last night in the park. I could really go for you, Terrace, really go for you hard."

"Brad . . . I . . ."

"But I have to cool it with you, honey. Oh, sure, I could lead you on. In fact, I was all set to do that when I suggested you stay on for a while in Dublin. I wanted to keep you here for as long as I have to stay so that I could . . . well, so that I could enjoy you. But . . . you're not in the cards for me, baby. I can't lose sight of . . . well, what I planned to go after."

"Brad . . ."

"You're mixing it all up. As I said, I could lead you on. Yet, for once in my life, I'd like to do it right. You're an angel, Terrace. I could really fall hard. You look and act and think like the gal I've been waiting for all my life."

"But it's just not the right timing?" she asked, still trying to find insight to the point he was trying to make.

"Oh, timing means nothing. It's just . . . it's just that I'm out for higher stakes."

She looked at him, not believing what she had thought she heard.

"You mean . . . you like me, everything about me . . . but . . ."

"Look, maybe you're right about timing. You're just out of school . . . a naive little angel . . . If I had

131

met you in five or ten years, when you were established . . ."

She looked at him blankly. Never until she took this trip did she realize how lacking she was in . . . well, according to Sheila she was lacking in style, and to Kevin, she was lacking in propriety and now Brad felt she was merely a little mouse just out of school and far from an established cosmopolitan woman of affluence and position. My, she thought, how could she have existed so long in life being such a nobody? And yet, with each attack against her, something had been changing within her. Instead of being beaten down and feeling utterly humble, she was suddenly coming through feeling stronger than she had been before.

"Bradford Ainsley," she said.

"Look, honey, I'm sorry."

And then she started to laugh. She had been so upset at the thought of telling this man that perhaps they should cool it, as she knew she didn't care for him as much as he might have cared for her. And now he was telling her she was not up to standards in his book.

"Now what's so funny," he said watching her cackle across from him.

"I was just thinking, Brad. What makes you think that if I were a little more established, as you put it, I would want to be sitting across from you having lunch?"

"Look, honey, I know you're sore, but I just wanted to be honest with you."

"There's one thing that I realize, Brad. With everyone telling me what I'm not, I'm certainly beginning to know what I am. It was a very good idea for Aunt

Agatha to have sent me on this trip. The fog is lifting, Brad. For once in my life I know what and who I am. The slings and arrows directed at me since I've been here haven't worn me down at all. They've made me stronger within myself. I'm leaving now, Brad."

"Well, wait, at least let's finish our lunch," he stammered.

"Why?" she answered, rising from her chair. "I've no interest being here with you. Only came in the first place not to hurt your feelings. I've a few important things to do."

And she thought of those things as she made her way alone along the streets that would take her back to Merrion Square. She was sure that she wouldn't stay on too much longer in Ireland, but she did want to accomplish a few things before she left. The most important thing, of course, was to establish definitely if Moira could communicate with another person. And aside from this, she wanted, somehow, but the method was still vague to her, to help get Padrig established in his own business.

These two things were very important to her and that was the reason she did not hesitate to go directly up to her aunt's room as soon as she arrived in the house. She realized as she was mounting the stairs that she could very easily allow herself to become furious with herself for going to lunch with Brad at all. Yet she decided to dismiss all thought of him for the time being and concentrate on her aunt.

Moira was sitting comfortably in the four-poster with three pillows propped up against her back. She looked serene and cozy to Terrace as she entered the bedroom. Lizbeth had been reading aloud to her and without changing the inflection of her voice, acknowledged Terrace's entrance with a nod of her head.

Terrace stood just inside the doorway to the room and listened while Lizbeth finished the paragraph she was reading. The scene was so peaceful that she wondered if she had the right to interrupt what seemed to be a restful afternoon for her aunt in order to work on the communication theory with her.

"Miss Connors," Lizbeth smiled, having come to a pause in her reading. "It's so good of you to stop in to see your aunt again. Your luncheon appointment was a short one, was it?"

"Ah . . . yes . . . yes it was. I wonder, Lizbeth. Do you think it would be too much for Moira if I talked with her awhile?"

"Oh, I should say not, miss. She is doing very well, and the outing didn't affect her stamina at all. She ate well, here in her room, and took a short nap. I'm sure she would be delighted if you sat with her, now wouldn't you, Mistress Moira?"

Terrace saw the older woman lift her index finger once to indicate an affirmative response, but of course Lizbeth had no knowledge of this.

"Ah, poor mistress. If you could only answer, I know you would say that you are pleased at your niece's visit," Lizbeth went on chattering as she straightened the pillows for Moira and prepared to leave the room.

"I won't take that long with her, Lizbeth," the girl said as she made herself comfortable in the chair that Lizbeth had just vacated.

"Never you mind now, miss. Take as long as you

like. She is most happy that you are here," the servant said as she left the room.

"Is that true, aunt? Are you happy that I'm visiting you?"

The older woman's eyes shone brightly as her index finger indicated the pleasure of seeing her niece.

"I was in the Center for a little while today, Moira," she said, not wanting to pressure the woman immediately into the communication bit. "I enjoy walking through the Center. As a matter of fact, one of these days soon, I must walk farther over to see the bay. It will remind me of home, I imagine. I live near a bay, too, Aunt Moira—San Francisco Bay. Oh, it's beautiful there, aunt. It's a grand city of many hills and elegant homes. Everywhere you go, there are Victorian buildings sporting bay windows—and from practically every house you can see snatches of the bay and of the bridges that span it.

"Of course, some of the homes are more elegant than others. Ours . . . or I should say Aunt Agatha's, is not the most costly of homes, but it is very comfortable and homey.

"What is it, aunt? I seem to see—there's a tear dropping down your cheek. Something I have said upset you? Yes? But what could it be? Something about the fact that my home was modest? Yes? Oh, but Aunt Moira—it is nothing that should make you sad."

The woman's finger reverted from one lifting to two, and Terrace watched for a short while, suddenly terrified that the theory of her aunt's communication was not a reality. She felt herself tensing, as she so wanted her theory to be correct.

"You . . . are sorry, but then you're not about my

135

Chapter 11

She looked at herself in the mirror of the vanity, but her face was not in its image. Instead she saw Bradford Ainsley across the table at lunch that afternoon, picking away at his food, trying to keep up with her light conversation until he finally made his statement to her. Terrace Connors was not good enough for Bradford Ainsley. He was after higher stakes.

She laughed at herself as her mirror image returned once more to her eyes. It was lucky that she had decided to leave Ireland and return home instead of . . . oh, admit it, Terrace, instead of staying and trying to make a play for Kevin. If she didn't fit into the plan that Brad thought he deserved, then surely it would be a mockery to think that someone like Kevin would be interested in her. She was attracted to Kevin—very much so—but it was not meant to be, she shrugged, as she began brushing her hair. If there had been any hope at all with Kevin, Sheila surely squelched that by showing all present what an unsophisticated country mouse Terrace was. Not that she felt that way, of course.

Again she thought of the statement she had made to Brad. Living in the shadow of Aunt Agatha—dear Aunt Agatha, and she felt as close to her as ever now—yet living in her shadow, never made her realize that she could stand on her own. And now, once away from the house with the porch and the bay windows, she felt as though she was strong within herself. Of course, it was not pleasant to be visiting a house where most of the inhabitants disliked her. Inner strength could not eliminate the uncomfortable feelings that stirred within her when Sheila remarked about her lack of taste in clothing or when Brad admitted that she lacked enough stature for him to spend any more time courting. The remarks did make her wince, but not cower in humble resignation either. She looked forward to getting back to San Francisco and beginning her work in interior decorating. She may not be an important enough person to Brad, but she was important to herself—and the knowledge of this was new and exciting to her.

There would be only one true regret when she left Dublin, and that was the fact that Kevin had misunderstood her reason for being there. That was unfair of him, of course, but then the man was also ridden with grief over his deceased wife and other problems within the household. The other was not his fault— after all, it was not his problem or doing that she had fallen in love with the man.

She stood up and looked at her image. She wondered if Sheila would approve of this dress at least. It was a dark brown silk with a plain but low-necked bodice and long tapering sleeves. Somber, she thought. Somber like her own mood. The pendant falling well past the edge of the neckline gave it all a very dramatic air.

It was a little early to gather for the pre-dinner cocktail they were all accustomed to, but she thought she would venture down to the study anyway. More time in her room would only lead her to think more of Kevin. She knew there would be no hope for them on a serious level, but the fact that he thought she was there for her own gain was almost harder to digest.

"Off to the study with you, Miss Connors," she said aloud to the mirror. "Perhaps you and Padrig could get into a verbal battle to pass the time away before the others assemble."

But it wasn't Padrig Corot who was already in the study. To her dismay, she found Kevin Sanford serving a glass of sherry to an unidentified man. She stopped short at the study entrance, feeling foolish for having interrupted them.

"No, Terrace, do come in," Kevin beckoned her with a wave of his hand and no apparent emotion or lack of it in his voice.

"I could come back," she said quietly.

"It's not necessary. There are no secrets here. As a matter of fact, this is a good opportunity for you to meet Dr. Canavan, Moira's physician. Dr. Canavan, this is Terrace Connors, Moira's niece."

"Ah, yes, Miss Connors. Kevin was telling me that you brought Moira into the air today. I was quite pleased to hear that. You may do so again on any day that is as lovely as this one."

"Well, I'll give your suggestion to Lizbeth, Dr. Canavan. I'll . . . I'll just be here for a few more days. I'm going back to the States, you see."

"So soon? I thought Kevin mentioned that you just arrived."

"It has been a pleasant visit, though short," she answered, purposefully not looking at Kevin, knowing that he was now gaping at her. Padrig had not mentioned to Kevin, then, that she had threatened to leave. This was the first that Kevin was hearing of it. He should be pleased, she guessed. He had never wanted her to stay in the first place.

"I'm sorry to hear that, Miss Connors. I know Moira is enjoying your visit," the doctor said.

She didn't answer, and behind her Kevin was now asking what she wanted to drink.

"Sherry would be fine," she said over her shoulder, still not meeting his eyes.

"But she is holding her own, then, Doctor?" Kevin asked as he filled her glass.

"Oh, yes. I've told you already that she had regained partial use of some fingers."

"Yes, Nora said she had been working on therapy in that area," Kevin answered as he gave Terrace the glass of sherry without looking directly at her.

"Well, she must have worked very hard with Moira, because her fingers are moving."

"She said—Nora, that is—that she had a lot of things in mind for Moira using the therapy. I never did learn what these were. She said she was going to inform the rest of the family later with all areas of progress—sort of a surprise she was planning. We never learned what all these plans were. She . . . passed away before she could tell us."

"A pity. We'll have to get a therapist in this summer, Kevin, a permanent one. The therapy sessions that I've provided have worked well. Lizbeth is doing a fine job, but I'd like to have a steady professional for a while. I have a feeling it will work wonders."

"Feel free to prescribe anything you'd like," Kevin answered.

Terrace knew that this would be the time to mention Moira's ability to communicate. And yet, was she sure she knew that Moira was capable of this? Dr. Canavan and Kevin, she could hear herself saying, Moira and I spoke to each other today. No, that would not do. Should she tell them now, or have one more go at it with Moira, she wondered.

"I'm not worried about Moira, Kevin," the doctor was continuing. "I'm a little worried about you, though."

"What do you mean, Doctor?" Kevin was facing the doctor now, a perplexed look on his face.

"I . . . I did tell you that there was little hope of complete normal mobility."

"Yes, I know that, Doctor."

"Do you, Kevin? I mean, do you understand that? And speaking . . . if she ever speaks again, it won't happen for a long while, if ever."

"Yes, we've gone over this. I do understand all that. I wonder why you mention it now."

"It's . . . well, the phone calls, Kevin. I don't mind the calls coming in . . . it's just . . . my nurse has told me that you call quite often—checking and rechecking the prognosis. There's nothing more definite that I could tell you. Oh, and there's also been a woman calling . . . ah . . . checking the same thing," the doctor said.

The glare between Kevin and Terrace took only a short time, but it was there, strong, accusing, uncertain, but definite.

"Yes, well . . ." Kevin turned his attention back to the doctor. "I guess we're just concerned for her, Doctor," he stammered.

142

"I realize that," Dr. Canavan said quickly. "And, Kevin, you've been a rock through all this. You've kept the family together. You've borne the brunt of the responsibility on top of your own personal loss."

"It's nothing," Kevin said almost inaudibly.

"Why don't you get away from here for a while, lad. Take a short trip, change the atmosphere."

"Yes . . . well, I was thinking of doing something like that, actually." He was still facing the doctor, but Terrace saw that a smile had crossed his face. "Thought of going to Paris for a short time," he said, still smiling like a small child about to embark on a prankish caper.

"Good. Paris would be good for you."

It was at that moment that the rest of the household began to descend upon the study. Pegeen arrived first, elegantly coiffed and dressed in a dark-green silk dress. Then, Padrig and Sheila, engaged in heated conversation which stopped abruptly at the door. The doctor shook hands with each of them and each time commented that he could not stay longer but had to hurry away for a previous appointment. He nodded a farewell to Terrace as he left the room.

The family gathered around the small bar as Kevin continued dispensing drinks. It was Pegeen who stood out from the group first, with glass in hand, taking a stance and looking directly at her niece.

"Terrace, where did you go off to this afternoon?" she seemed to bellow and all heads turned immediately to the girl seated on the divan.

"You mean . . . at lunchtime?"

"Yes," came the quick answer.

"I went to lunch with . . . Brad."

"Brad? Brad who?"

"Bradford Ainsley. He was at the reception. He knows a friend of Padrig's."

"Well, I haven't met him. You know, Terrace, you are living under this roof and are expected to conform to our social customs."

"Social customs? I don't quite understand, Pegeen."

"Obviously you don't, my dear. The women in this family have usually introduced their young men when they came to call or to escort them somewhere. Now you may be used to a more . . . loose arrangement in your upbringing, but we have social obligations to live up to here. We are a very good, well-bred family . . . or most of us are, anyway."

"I'm sorry, Pegeen. I don't think it will happen again," she said quietly, praying that the flush she felt covering her face was not too apparent to the others.

"Pegeen, go easy on poor Terrace. I know I'm not family," Sheila cooed, "but I'm sure she's trying her best. By the way dear Terrace, where did you get that devastating dress? My, my, such a sophisticated cut, and you said you had nothing left over from your parents' lives. Surely you salvaged that from your mother's wardrobe. What a kicky idea. I must ask Mom if she has any discards. An entire new fad could be started here."

"I'm happy you like it, Sheila," she said looking straight at her while noticing that Kevin and Padrig were staring straight down into their drinks.

"Lizbeth tells me that you had Moira out this morning," Pegeen continued.

"Yes, the weather was so lovely that I . . ."

"Henceforth, Terrace, I wish you would check with

144

me first before changing the pattern of the household. My dear, we must do something about you. I imagine you've been on your own so long that your show of courtesy to your elders has been utterly neglected."

"Oh, Mother, I saw Terrace outside with Moira. She was making her quite happy," cut in Padrig whose upper lip was beginning to show perspiration.

"Not the point, Padrig. Not the point at all. If we do anything for Terrace this summer it's to groom her to fit properly into given circumstances," she answered her son. "Why, Terrace, where are you off to now?" she gasped as her niece rose from the divan, placed her glass on the small table in front of it and began to walk toward the door.

"I'm sure you could do a lot with me to add some polish to my life, Pegeen," she said over her shoulder. "Yet the one thing you can't do at the moment is to restore my loss of appetite. If you will excuse me," she said. As she passed through the doorway she heard her aunt heave a loud sigh of exasperation accompanied by a background giggle which she was positive came from Sheila.

The tears stung her face as she walked as slowly and as stately as possible up the tall staircase. She tarried in her room only long enough to pull her trench coat out of the closet and finished donning it as she retraced her steps to the lower front foyer. She could not be seen from the study and took a few minutes to fasten the belt of her coat and pull a scarf from its pocket to tie around her head.

"Miss Connors," came the whisper from the far hallway which led to the kitchen. "Is there something wrong? Are you not staying for dinner, miss?"

"No, Lizbeth. Please don't set a place for me. I've decided to . . . I'm going to take a walk by the bay."

"Oh, miss. That is quite far from here, and the night has turned misty. Such a pity after the wonderful day we had."

"I'll be all right, Lizbeth. In San Francisco I lived near a bay. I could merely open the window and smell the sea and feel calm. I've missed it. The walk won't be that long and it will do me good."

"I don't know, miss. Why don't I get Padrig or Mr. Sanford to accompany you?"

"Please don't, Lizbeth, and don't even mention where I've gone. I just need a time for myself. You understand, don't you?"

"Yes . . . I imagine so, Miss Connors."

The wetness of the air hit her body as soon as the door to the house closed behind her. It was as if she had no coat on at all as the dampness seeped under it and already her skin felt chilled. She looked down at her shoes and realized that she had not even bothered to change from her brown sandals, her haste had been so great to leave her surroundings. She wouldn't bother to return now at the expense of facing them, any one of them. The sandals were comfortable and although their heels were high, she had always considered them as easy lounge shoes. They clicked now as she made her way left on the old cobblestones that would lead her to the sea. The echo of her journey seemed to resound loudly through the empty streets whose buildings now faded into the gray mist like people withdrawing from the gloomy night.

She seemed to be the only one about, the only soul that sought comfort and warmth outside of the hearth.

The family at Merrion Square would be content now, eating souffled potatoes and beef and drinking wine from Waterford goblets while seated around the elegantly set dinner table. Their conversation would be accompanied by the flicker of flames maneuvering their red and yellow fingers through the ample supply of firewood that Lizbeth had placed in the bosom of the stone hearth. What would their conversation consist of, she wondered—these people that were her family or as close to a family as she ever imagined. Would they be speaking of her . . . of the orphaned waif whose only claim to sophistication was the fact that she grew up in a sophisticated and exciting city? None of them seemed to feel that the sophistication of the city had rubbed off on her.

She marveled again on how she never had lacked anything in her life until the people on Merrion Square pointed it all out to her—though she still couldn't digest the image they were trying to insinuate she was. As a child, her days were never lonely, although there were not that many children in the neighborhood. If she were not playing with the two or three children who lived within the four-block radius of Aunt Agatha's house, she would be busy with Agatha herself. They were constantly discovering new recipes or cutting out skirt patterns that might be used at an upcoming church social. There had never been any pressure from Agatha to become someone she was not. Therefore, she had never felt there was anything lacking in herself. Growing up had all been made very natural to her. Perhaps she should not have been made so comfortable. Perhaps she should have been made aware of what others had in order to strive farther than the bounds of what Aunt Agatha could provide. And yet she had always felt that she had as much as anyone else. She had love and contentment and peace—until a few minutes ago. And then her peace had exploded and she had been humiliated enough to stalk out of the house, completely enraged. Still, it had not really been anger that had made her leave.

She was tired—tired of Padrig using her for his personal aims; tired of Pegeen insinuating that her upbringing made her the unpolished member of the family; tired of Sheila putting her down and planting a seed in Kevin's mind that her taste in clothes was lacking and her general background was worse than seedy. And finally, she was tired of Kevin, with his resentment of her, with his coldness toward her, with his suspicion that she had descended upon the household for monetary gains. She was tired of him and yet he held her in some mesmerized state, waiting for the token of his smile, hoping for a thaw in his emotions. And there she was, the strong Terrace Connors, who had left a dismal lunch with Brad, knowing who she was, untouched by anyone's criticism—having been humiliated enough to stalk out of the room and out of the house on Merrion Square. No, she was still strong—if it had not been for Kevin . . . if Kevin had not seen her humiliated.

Quickly her mind turned toward the doctor who had been with Kevin when she had entered the study. Was Kevin really calling the doctor's office at frequent intervals to inquire about Moira? The doctor sounded as though he thought it strange that Kevin should inquire so often. Of course, he was concerned about Moira. But what if it wasn't that at all? Kevin had not worked in a long while, or so Padrig had mentioned. Then why was he merely lingering at the house on Merrion Square. Could he, after all, be a fortune hunter, waiting to get from Moira, after her demise, enough subsistence to set him up comfortably for life? And what of the woman who had called the doctor's office. Of course, Kevin had looked at her so accusingly after the doctor had made that statement that she was sure he had thought it had been she who had made the call. Was he thinking—as he always had—that she was checking on Moira's condition with the same dishonest thought in mind? And yet, his glance at her could have meant that he was merely mortified that she had heard any of the conversation by the doctor—the conversation that led her strongly to believe that Kevin and a woman—Sheila?—were making constant and unnecessary inquiries, therefore frantic inquiries, on Moira's health.

Enough, she thought. Enough of family embroilment. Enough even of Kevin. She would never again allow her mind to wander in his direction. She would never again permit her body to churn within as she longed for his touch. Instead, she would leave Dublin in two days, she decided. She would spend one more day with Moira and then contact Dr. Canavan to mention her discovery of her aunt's ability to communicate. Then she would leave. She would leave without even contacting Agatha that she would be returning. She would merely arrive on the doorstep and in a few moments Agatha would know. She would know that Terrace Connors, twenty-one and a recent graduate of the School of Interior Design, had had enough.

She had long left the center of the city when the

149

road had divided giving the choice of going farther into the country or up a steep incline that would lead to the sea. As she made her way up the hill, the wind howled unmercifully around her and she raised the collar of her trench coat in an effort to keep warmer. And yet the flush that was beginning in her face was not from warmth of the collar that now covered the lower portion of her face, but from the anger that began to seep through her body.

It was then that the thought entered her mind that she would be leaving Dublin in complete defeat. Pegeen would have her feelings toward her reconfirmed while Sheila would gloat and Kevin would be pleased. And Padrig? Padrig would be sorry at her departure . . . sorry that his purpose for having her there was not fulfilled. Still, that disappointment would be selfish on Padrig's part and not any show of empathy for her. She would get back at them all, she thought. She would tell them that the trip was not her idea. She would tell them that she had never wanted to leave San Francisco. She had wanted no part in either taking over the household or reaping any financial benefits from the estate. She would tell them . . . nothing. There would be no use to go into a hurt child's tirade. And after all, she would not leave as defeated as all that. Moira would have a voice through the use of her fingers. And after she told Dr. Canavan of Moira's possible ability to communicate, Moira would have better days. So there was something that would come of her journey to Dublin, even if that had no personal bearing on her own life.

The road was at its steepest now as the mist closed in around Terrace almost entirely. Yet through the thick snatches of white cloud, she could see parts of the rocky ledge that led from the road to the beach. And once or twice she even saw the white foam of the choppy gray water thrashing its way to the sand. Through all of it came the magnificent aroma of the sea and she stood still a moment to breathe its essence. Nostalgic scenes of the Pacific ran through her mind. And she would have allowed the nostalgia to continue, sweet and protective, had her senses not awakened her into a sharp realization. The wind and the small crescendo of waves from the beach receded into the background to give precedence to a more prominent sound. Not far along the road she had just traversed came the obvious echo of solid footsteps, steady and determined. Of course she realized that the road was not her own private way and could be used by anyone from the city. Yet something in the sound of the steps seemed to warn her that they were heading straight and deliberately for her.

Chapter 12

She stood very still for a moment, annoyed that her newfound solace might soon be interrupted. Of course, no one would be coming for her, she thought. She had told Lizbeth not to tell anyone at the house where she was headed. Surely Lizbeth would not have betrayed her request. Yet the girl had seemed worried. She had wanted to send Padrig or Kevin to walk with her. Dear, concerned Lizbeth. At least there had been one member of the household who had been courteous to her. Could that courteousness now backfire on her? Would Lizbeth have gone to Kevin or Padrig and told them of her concern? Still, if the person walking the road was anyone from the house, it would probably be Padrig, stalking her as he did in the Center the other day. Padrig, who was making doubly sure that she would not disappear into thin air before she had completed her usefulness to him. Poor Padrig. Poor lost Padrig. Why was she lashing out at him now, making him the brunt of her unhappiness?

But of course it would be Padrig. Why would Kevin ruin his dinner to come after her in this dense mist?

She brushed away a strand of hair that the wind had blown across her face. Whoever it was, she thought, it had better be some stranger from the town. She wanted to see none of the people from Merrion Square. She wanted to think that none of them had come to fetch her as they would a small child who had become petulant and stalked out of the house.

"Terrace. Terrace Connors," were the words she heard bellowed by the deep resounding voice from the far end of the road. "Terrace," it continued as her muscles tensed and flexed as an animal would when prewarned of danger.

Kevin, why does it have to be you, she said almost audibly. She thought of Kevin telling Dr. Canavan that he was thinking of taking a trip to Paris. She thought of Kevin looking provocatively at Sheila Malloy, complimenting her on how she looked. And she thought of Kevin and how he would look when he found her, mocking her that she should have acted so childish as to stalk out of the house at dinnertime.

"Terrace, if you are there, please call out to me," he bellowed again, and she knew that he would be almost upon her soon. Yet the mist and fog were very thick, and if she moved quickly, she would be able to gain distance.

She turned immediately, and careful not to make too much noise with her heels, she began groping her way forward away from his voice. The road had long ago narrowed and now she noticed that there was no pavement at all under her shoes. Either the road had ended abruptly, or the mist had confused her sense of direction and she had ventured onto an area of grass and rocks and boulders. She heard the thrashing of the waves along the beach, but the sound was no closer or farther than it had been earlier. She could only move inches at a time, as she could see nothing beyond the next step in her footing. She would try to make it back to the house and up to her room without encountering anyone.

And it was with this determination in mind that she had placed her foot down on the hard core of boulder in front of her only to realize too late that the surface of the rock, made slippery by the mist, would repel the high heel of her shoe. She wrenched her body spasmodically to keep herself from the inevitable fall that was coming, but there was no way to catch herself. As she swung upward, she felt her ankle turn and its pain was only overshadowed by the throbbing in her arm as she maneuvered it to hit the rock first, thus preventing possible damage to her head. She was stunned at first, and then she moaned quietly as both her arm and foot sent prickles of pain throughout the rest of her body.

Her left arm lay limp at her side and her right hand clutched her right knee to her chest, pulling at it to try to relieve the pain that shot up from her foot. Her coat and dress, torn and stained with mud, were above her thighs now and her hair hung wildly over her face as the tears stung at her cheeks. It was in this disarray that she saw him as his tall massive frame loomed up before her, cutting the mist into swirling cloud.

She could do nothing but whimper as she looked up at him, feeling that nothing he could say to her now could cause her more pain than she was feeling at that moment. He stared at her only for a moment before he began to move. He was taking off his own trench coat and rolling it in a ball before he was beside her. He urged her to lay back on the same boulder that had felled her while he used his coat as a pillow for her head.

"Terrace, what has happened to you? Where are you hurt?" he asked as he leaned over her, using his hand to brush away the hair from her face.

"My foot . . . and arm . . . the boulder was wet," she gasped, more now from the closeness of his body than from the wretchedness of her painful limbs.

"Did you hit your head at all?" he whispered, and now his face was merely centimeters away from hers.

"No . . . it's just my arm and my ankle," she answered.

"Do you realize that you're at the edge of the cliff? If you had fallen in a different position, you would have gone hurtling down the cliffside." he snapped.

The tears that had momentarily subsided began to flow down her cheeks again and she could not control the whimper that escaped her lips.

"Terrace, oh, Terrace, my darling," was all he said before he was fully on the ground beside her pulling her gently, but firmly, against him. "I would die if I lost you now," he said, his voice low and husky with emotion. His lips held an urgency as he sought her mouth, allowing his hands to slip inside her coat so that he could bring her firmly to him. The throbbing in her reached a different peak now. As she felt the overwhelming tremor in his body and listened to his heavy breaths of longing, she let everything slip from her mind and surrendered into an uncaring reverie of ecstasy.

She lay against his chest as he stroked her hair and caressed her back with his massive hands.

"You won't ever do that again, promise?" he whispered in her ear.

"Never do what, Kevin?"

"Never do anything without asking me first."

She laughed. "I couldn't stay in the house anymore. Pegeen and . . ." She was about to say Sheila, but refused to mention her name.

"We've got a lot to talk about, Terrace. But my first concern is to get you back to your room. I'm only happy that I was able to pry your whereabouts out of Lizbeth."

"You mean that she didn't come seeking you out asking you to follow me?"

"You must be joking. It was bad enough having to corner her in the kitchen, threatening her with extinction unless she told me where you were going."

"You asked for me, then?"

"Of course I asked for you. When you weren't in your room, I went immediately to Lizbeth."

She lifted her face to him, and looked into his troubled eyes. "Oh, Kevin. And I thought . . ."

"What did you think, Terrace?" he asked looking down at her.

She could never tell him all of the wild suspicions that had filled her mind before she fell. Yet there were many things that she wanted to ask him. "I thought . . . oh, Kevin, I don't know what I thought," she said, as she saw him smile down at her. Then his face clouded with emotion and his lips were pressing over her hair and her eyes and as he found her mouth, she could feel his desire for her well up in him again.

"I've got to get you home, Terrace," he said as he pushed her gently away from him. They looked fully at one another and then they both laughed as they realized how difficult it was for each of them to leave the other's side.

"Kevin, I don't think I will be able to make it," she said as she tried to pull herself to a sitting position.

"Nonsense. I'll help you make it," he answered as he scooped her up into his arms.

"What are you going to do?"

"I'm going to carry you off the sea road, at least. When we reach the fork, I'm sure we'll be able to flag down a car to drive us to the house. It will be slow going, but we'll make it. I used to play on this road as a child. I don't think we'll have too much trouble."

And they didn't. As she rested in bed later, having been totally washed and pampered by Lizbeth, she thought of his slow but determined mission in carrying her away from the road and back toward the center of town. They ran into no one at the fork and he had to carry her farther into the Center before they spotted a taxi which they took the rest of the way.

No one had been downstairs when they entered the house, and Kevin had carried her directly to her room before he summoned Lizbeth to administer to her. The girl had then bandaged her foot and placed her arm in a sling, the latter being merely bruised and nothing more.

Now as she lay under what she surmised was a dozen comforters, she thought of how drastic her thoughts had become before she fell on the cliff. She longed to see Kevin again. Longed to have him reaffirm in her mind that everything would be all right between them. And yet . . . there were so many questions left.

The knock on her door came soon after she had been made comfortable. As he entered, she noticed that his broad smile quickly overshadowed the natural serious expression on his face. The furrowed lines, now almost made permanent from his years of worry and sadness, softened immediately into the wide grin, and she felt her body melt at his overwhelming attractiveness.

"You do look a little less battered than an hour ago," he laughed as he pulled the single chair away from her vanity and placed it next to her side by the bed.

"Thanks to you, I think I'll recover," she answered as she raised her hand and allowed her fingers to touch his forehead and trace the lines along his cheeks.

He took her hand then and kissed it gently, but his grasp on her wrist was firm and demanding, and she knew that his longing on the cliff was no fantasy. "What made you run from the house, Terrace? I can't help but think that it could have been your end if you had gone over that cliff," he said, his face clouding again.

"I couldn't stay here anymore, Kevin. I couldn't listen to Pegeen putting me down and . . . Sheila slicing at me with every opportunity. I needed air. I needed to smell the sea."

"Well, their antics were predictable after this afternoon. I'm to blame for not foreseeing their pattern of attack and not preparing you for it. Actually, all this would not have happened if I hadn't left you to be the last to be told."

"Is there something wrong, Kevin?"

"Hope not," he said and he looked into her eyes directly, almost a little shyly.

"What is it?" she asked.

He didn't answer for a moment, then he stood up

and began to pace the floor, his hands embedded deeply in the pockets of his sport jacket. "I . . . took Sheila to lunch this afternoon."

"Yes, I know," she said quietly.

"I wanted to straighten out a few things with her."

"I see," she said. She felt her body tense.

"I wanted to tell her that I was in love with you, Terrace," he stopped in his pacing then and looked over his shoulder at her, his face coloring slightly. "I know, I know," he continued as he made his way over to the chair again to sit next to her. "Kind of a funny thing to be the last to hear, isn't it, Terrace?" he said as he lifted her hands into his. "But I wanted to straighten everything with Sheila."

"You wanted to end things with her?" she asked.

"End things? No. There was nothing to end. But I knew she was interested, very interested. I thought it would be only kinder . . ."

"Since you were both in Paris together and all?" she bit her lip, realizing that she was acting very much like a nagging wife.

"Oh, that?" He smiled. "Are you jealous, Terrace? Do you care for me at all to be jealous?"

Again she felt the pressure of his hands on her arms, and the tenseness in her relaxed as his apparent longing mixed with her own. He could never be close enough, she thought.

"On one of my trips to Paris . . ."

"No, don't tell me, Kevin. I had no right to ask that."

"There's not much to tell. On one of my trips to Paris I did run into Sheila at the airport. We sat on the plane together. I had a meeting with a publisher there and returned by dinnertime. I did notice that Sheila started coming over to the house more often after that. Along with her insinuations and actions, I felt that I wanted to straighten out her thinking before I talked to you. Even though, in the back of my mind, I thought you would not have me."

"You didn't know, Kevin, how I felt?"

"I thought at one point, as we were on our way to transport Moira . . . but I wasn't sure. My mind has been clouded with many things, Terrace."

"You've had a terrible burden here. And then, Padrig and Sheila both mentioned that you've had some business problems," she said as she released her hand from his and ran her fingers through his hair.

"Did they now?" he said and laughed. "Why did they mention that?"

"Padrig just mentioned it in passing. Sheila said that you were in banking and then when Nora died, you went into writing."

"Oh, I see. Well, my ability to be close-mouthed paid off, if they think that. I was writing for a long time although I always had a banking background. I did a lot of articles and short stories which didn't amount to much financially, yet I loved it. When . . . when Nora's father passed away and I felt responsible for her future, I reverted back to banking. I had to, Terrace. I had a responsibility then. All the while, though, I kept writing. After Nora's accident I still wrote and finally sold something big. As a matter of fact, a publishing house in New York bought it. Came out two months ago—a suspense yarn with a lot of background on banking in it."

"Two months ago?" she stammered. "You don't write under the name of K. G. Sanford, do you?"

"Yes, that's me," he chuckled quietly.

"But, Kevin, that book is already a best seller."

"My agent tells me it's doing pretty well," he smiled.

"You're . . . so unassuming about the whole thing."

"I'm just . . . a shy guy, Terrace," he said as his face became serious. "Very shy, and very much in love with you," he said, his voice now deep with emotion. It was no time before she felt his arms around her, scooping her up from the pillows, while she allowed the strength of his body and the desire of his mouth to overpower her.

"Kevin . . . that time on the landing, going to Moira's room," she whispered, "you did read me correctly?"

"I wanted it to be so, Terrace," he said as he pushed her gently back against the pillows again. "But you cooled."

"I thought that you and Sheila . . ."

"Sheila unfortunately is a mass of misinformation at times. Yet, that's not fair to her either. I could see how she thought I was having business problems—watching me go from being a banker, which would impress someone like Sheila—to merely sitting around the house batting out words on a typewriter. I never told anyone here about my book. And, the few people who have passed through from the States never connected K. G. Sanford with Kevin Sanford."

"Then . . ." she hesitated and yet knew it had to be

said. "You were so concerned about the estate. It couldn't be anything personal on your part, as that book of yours far surpasses anything that would come from this house."

"You thought I had my claws into inheritance here, I know. No, don't feel badly about it. The thought crossed my mind about you also. Terrace, there's so much to talk about. In a nutshell, it didn't matter to me where I did my writing. The reason I chose this place is that I didn't like Padrig's antics while I was living here with Nora. He gambles quite a bit, and a lot of Moira's money had already gone into bailing him out of trouble. With Moira in the condition she was in, I felt responsible for staying on a bit. Padrig has been very edgy lately. I've seen his edginess before when he's been badly in need of money."

"And the reason you were so against my staying was that you thought I was after Moira's estate?"

"No, not really, Terrace. I was too confused to tell you the truth. Then when I learned you were Greg Connors's daughter, I did everything I could think of to force you to leave. I was afraid that Padrig's trouble—whatever it is this time—might make him desperate so that he might get to you somehow. I still don't know what I was afraid of, but I had an uncanny feeling that he would involve you."

"You knew my father, then, Kevin?" she asked.

"The 'G' in K. G. Sanford is for Gregory. Your father was my godfather. Our parents knew each other very well. You are very like him, you know. Headstrong and feisty and as gentle as a lamb. I saw how gentle you were while tending to Moira in the garden." He was about to reach for her again when there was a quick knock and the door burst open to reveal a very efficient but perturbed Lizbeth who came clattering across the room.

"Now, Master Sanford. I know you let me have it earlier in the kitchen when I wouldn't tell you at first where Miss Connors had gone. But you'll be getting the same from me except double the amount if you don't leave this poor child alone. I have hot soup I'll be taking to her and she is to eat it alone. You are to leave now . . . come, come, come," she said as she took hold of his arm and practically lifted him from his seat.

"I have a lot to tell you, Kevin," Terrace put in before Lizbeth had escorted him half way across the room.

"Tomorrow, Terrace," he said, looking from the girl in the bed to the servant who was pulling him toward the door.

At one point Terrace thought he would explode at Lizbeth, but then his face softened and he shrugged and shook his head in amazement. Lizbeth turned toward Terrace as she was almost out the door with the man and gave an exaggerated wink of her eye.

Chapter 13

Lizbeth was true to her word and returned in a short while with a tray containing a bowl of steaming hot broth. She propped Terrace up comfortably against an army of pillows and would have spoon-fed the girl herself if she had not protested vehemently. After a few more moments of maternal fussing, Lizbeth left and Terrace was able to sip her broth slowly while lost in a world of her own, thinking of Kevin and wallowing in a newfound contentment.

The most important enlightenment to her was the fact that Kevin had not hovered around the house after Nora's death waiting for Moira to succumb so that he could benefit by the estate. In fact, her face began to flush at the thought of even having entertained such dreadful thoughts. Yet Kevin had believed the same of her when she first arrived. Then in knowing who she was he had tried to force her to leave as he envisioned that Padrig, in his desperation over money, would somehow get to her.

The soup was smooth and warming and slowly she felt her body restore itself to a normal state. Her arm was sore now, but nothing more, and although her ankle throbbed, the bandaging that Lizbeth expertly administered had lessened the initial agony. She felt content, except for a new desire in her to see Kevin once more before the end of the night.

How grand it was to know that this man cared for her! How marvelous it would be to spend the rest of her life with him. No, she was rushing ahead too far. She would have to be content at present in knowing that he cared for her, even desired her. She would not ruin things by having her mind race on. Although having already felt the strength of his arms and the tremor of his passion, she could not imagine how she could exist if these things were ever taken away from her. In thinking further, she wondered how she existed before, in a semi-state of life, half asleep before he had awakened her senses and anointed her body with love. She felt life so strongly now because of him.

She was so deep in thought that at first she heard, yet disregarded, the half echo of the telephone bell that sounded like a feeble sigh of exasperation, then her mind clicked off from its reverie and she was immediately aware of the fact that the ring was a signal of someone dialing out on another extension in the house.

It was very late at night for anyone to be up, and yet what did she actually know of the personal activities of anyone in the house? She was a guest there—a recent guest at that—and although it seemed an eternity had passed since her plane had landed at Dublin airport, it had been merely days that she had been there. What could she have learned about these people in her short time in Dublin? Even Kevin she had misunderstood until that very evening.

To think that she was accusing Kevin Sanford of hovering around Moira in order to reap from her estate. And all the while, Kevin, whose book had been immediately acclaimed as a best seller in the States, was lingering at the house to keep an eye on Moira and to be sure Padrig did not squander all the family's remaining funds.

No, she did not know these people well—neither their habits nor their activities. It could be anyone using the phone at that odd hour for any number of unimportant reasons, and yet she could not take her eyes off the apparatus on the other side of the room. And since she knew that she would get no rest with the question left unanswered in her mind, she put her wooden tray aside and threw off the covers.

She seriously hoped that no one would decide to pay her a visit at that point, as her maneuverings to reach the other side of the room with her injured limbs bordered on the comical. Yet her determination gave her all the incentive she needed and she finally reached the single chair next to the telephone table. She hated herself for what she was about to do, but some compulsion within made her lift the receiver.

"I know it's very late," Pegeen was saying, "but I had to call. Whoever thought you'd go soft?"

"She's too innocent, no, naive," said the other voice which was very distinct and very clear, and it was clearly the voice of Bradford Ainsley.

"But you were being paid well. I wanted her out of the house, away from the eyes of Moira—and especially out of contact with Kevin Sanford. Now you're leaving me high and dry."

"Listen, Pegeen, I just couldn't do it, don't you understand? I really never grasped why you wanted me to play out the part in the first place," he sighed.

"I wanted you to take her out, cavort around town, and the like. I didn't want her to get too close to

Moira. I didn't want her to take the place of that Nora. We have enough people waiting for Moira's estate without adding another contender to Moira on a silver platter."

"But Moira can't speak. How could she add Terrace to her will at this stage of the game?"

"That's just it, Brad. Moira's prognosis is very uncertain. She may just wake up one morning and be able to speak. That's why I wanted Terrace out of the way of her aunt."

"And Kevin. Why did you deliberately want me to steer her away from him?"

"Because Nora was the apple of Moira's eye. Now I'm sure in her passing, Moira would provide for Nora's husband. But Sheila would have taken care of that end. We made a deal, you see. Long ago, with a word from me, Sheila was able to embark on her career as a fashion coordinator. She likes the better things in life that girl—came from good stock with a lack of ready cash. She was attracted to Kevin, but she also knew that with his banking experience and a good-sized legacy from Moira, he would be a good catch for the future. If he did receive a good portion of the estate, she would have . . . shall we say, compensated me for my favor to her with her career. Now you've put a damper on my entire scheme, Brad. Who thought you'd choose love over money. Especially with your sordid background," Pegeen lamented.

"It wasn't love—yet. If I'd let it run its course, it could have easily reached that point. I just figured . . . for once in my life I should do something . . . straight. In this case, doing something straight was not having any part in your little scheme. Anyway, Pegeen, I'm not choosing love over money because I'm leaving for Amsterdam tomorrow morning. I've got something good going for me over there."

"Nonsense. I think you just went soft," Pegeen mumbled as if lost in some private incantation of disbelief. "That kind of woman always leaves an impression—willowy body, innocent look in her eyes—intelligent but naive. Her mother was the same. My brother lost his senses over her, otherwise he would not have married anyone out of his background. Now her daughter is having the same effect on Kevin. Sheila sensed that immediately. She had a difficult time, poor Sheila, trying to put the girl down at every opportunity while knowing that Kevin was becoming more and more interested in her. And now you—the biggest surprise of all."

"Listen," Brad's voice became harsh. "If I were giving up money for love, I'd stay here and fight for her. I thought of it, you know. But I had to come to terms with myself. Priorities you know. And I figured . . . there'll be other Terraces . . . well, hopefully there will be . . . later when I have enough money. Money is important to me, Pegeen, the way it seems to be for you."

She disregarded the last part. "Then why go all the way to Amsterdam to get it? You could have made a nice sum here," Pegeen retorted.

"Well . . . I owed the angel a good turn. She . . . touched me deeply. First time in a while. And Pegeen . . ."

"Yes?"

"She is an angel, you know. Go easy on her."

"Soft. You actually turned soft," Pegeen grunted.

"Maybe so. Anyway, see you, Pegeen," was the barely audible response before both parties hung up.

She placed her own receiver down in its cradle and sat back in the chair. The picture cleared so rapidly for her that she was almost breathless. Brad was working for Pegeen to help her solidify the receipt of at least something from Moira's estate. When was it that he began to feel remorseful about his assignment for Pegeen? Was it after he had held her in his arms that night in the park?

Her eyes closed as her distaste for the situation went through her in a shudder. Then for the next few minutes, she mustered all her energies into transporting herself back across the room. The feeling of the satin pillows and down-filled quilts comforted her and she stretched herself fully and luxuriously before her mind began working again.

She wondered if she had acquired some sixth sense which had prewarned her subconscious that Bradford Ainsley was not quite right for her. He had begun to waken her senses in the park, and yet something had made her draw away as she realized there existed no deep feeling in her for him. Yet things seemed to have turned out differently for Brad. He had told Pegeen that he could have fallen in love with her.

Poor Brad, she thought. By leaving Dublin he was being as much of a gentleman as he could muster.

Yet it was not Brad whom she should be thinking of now. It was her scheming aunt who should be receiving her thought waves. What desperation that woman must feel to pursue such a complicated yet childish scheme.

And suddenly Terrace was amused. So Sheila's constant putdowns were not an honest evaluation of her after all. According to Pegeen, Sheila had felt threatened by her presence. It had been wise on her part that she had not taken the criticism to heart.

The door opened slowly just then and as her name was called, she recognized Kevin's voice.

"Kevin, do come in please," she cried, her spirits lifting immediately.

"I didn't want to disturb you if you were asleep," he answered as he closed the door behind him.

"That's quite all right. I think I've become used to you barging in without knocking," she said and then they both laughed as they remembered his intrusion into her room the very first time they had met.

"I didn't know who you were at first on that day. I thought that Padrig had brought one of his friends in for a long stay—expecting Moira to house and feed her with no expense to Padrig," he explained as he brought a chair over to her bedside.

"Kevin, how did you know that I was longing to see you again tonight?"

"I'm merely good at knowing things like that," he said as his face clouded. "And, besides, the longing is very much on my part," he added just before he reached for her and she found herself being held very tightly in his massive arms while his mouth found hers quite ready to meet his demanding passion.

"Terrace, you know that I'll never be able to be away from you for too long a time," he said huskily as he helped her sit back comfortably against the pillows again.

"I felt that I just had to talk to you once more before the night was over," she said.

"Well, I did wait a while for Lizbeth to get to bed before I attempted a return visit. I wouldn't want to tangle with that one again. I think I'm really afraid of her," he laughed, and she soon joined him as they mused over the petite Lizbeth and her dictatorial tendencies.

"Kevin, would you think me terrible if I kept you up a good while longer tonight. I want to mention a few things that just can't wait until morning."

"Of course. A terribly bad habit to discover in one's future wife," he pouted exaggeratedly.

"Kevin . . . ?" she couldn't believe what she thought she had heard.

"Well, what do you expect? I told you. I think it's become an obsession with me. I must know that you'll be close to me for the rest of my life. Will you have me, Terrace?"

"I don't believe I could think of my future without you. Yet . . . I was afraid to hope," she answered.

"No, Terrace, that's what we must not lose sight of again and that is hope. I almost lost sight of it for a while."

"I really must talk to you, very seriously."

"Ah, yes. Back to keeping me up for the rest of the night. Try me and see how much it bothers me," he laughed.

It was easy to tell him everything that happened from the time Aunt Agatha told her she would be going to Dublin to her agitation before she stalked out of the house that evening. She decided that she would not mention the telephone conversation she had heard between Pegeen and Brad. As she was about to relate it, it all seemed so petty and really unimportant. And then when he made his next comment, she realized she would not be eliminating anything he did not know if she left it unmentioned.

"Good for Moira," he said. "With all the vultures in this house waiting for a part of the estate, she fools everyone by actually being able to communicate. I'm really thrilled over that. It not only proves that future therapy would probably have a positive effect on a greater number of muscles, but that Moira is alert enough to actually communicate intelligently. I'm really happy about this."

"I was going to tell the family, but I wanted to be sure I knew what I was talking about."

"Oh, I understand that. You must have been skeptical when you first discovered it," he said.

"I was really shocked, Kevin. But does that really mean that she has a better chance of recovery? I mean I know that you've been quite concerned. Dr. Canavan said that you've been checking on her a lot with his office," she bit her lip, realizing that this was the last bit of doubt within her concerning Kevin, and she wanted to clear it then before it festered at a later time.

He sighed a very deep and troubled sigh, and at first she was afraid that she had offended him.

"Terrace," he said as he sat back in his chair and resumed a very serious expression. "Are you really feeling up to staying awake a bit longer tonight?"

"I don't feel tired. I'm really fine. I'd much rather sit here with you than go to sleep."

"My Terrace," he said as he stroked her hair. "You're so overtired that you're wide awake. All right, then. You won't be able to sleep anyway. We'll just let you sleep later in the morning."

"But what is it that worried you when I mentioned Dr. Canavan's name?"

"There's one thing that disturbed me. You see, I didn't know what Dr. Canavan was talking about when he mentioned that I kept calling his office asking after Moira. I swear, Terrace, I haven't been calling the doctor's office."

"And I thought . . ." she stammered.

"Yes, you thought for a moment that I was waiting for Moira's estate—just as I thought you might have been the female who supposedly called once."

"You did think that? Even for a moment," she laughed.

"Of course, for a brief moment. One lives in a house of suspicions, and one becomes suspicious—even slightly."

"But, what does it all mean?" she asked.

"As long as you or I have not been calling, obviously waiting for part of the estate, then all of it means nothing—or nothing more than we know already. Padrig, Pegeen, and Sheila—yes, Sheila—are desperate to get their hands on money. It's nothing new—so it's not important."

"But . . . Kevin. Would they . . . I mean . . . ?"

"Would they harm Moira? No. These people are not that desperate or that complicated. Just chalk it up to family pettiness and bad budgeting."

"Yes, as I just mentioned to you, Moira has been upset about something. At first I thought she was just being emotional. I mean, after all these years, her brother's daughter—and a favorite brother, I'm told

173

here—anyway, her brother's daughter descends upon her bringing with the visit memories of long ago years, happy years when most of her family was alive and she was well."

"It could have been that, you know," he answered.

"No, Kevin. Really, it wasn't. It was something else. You're sure that no one here is harming her in any way."

"I'm pretty certain of that, Terrace. There's nothing really sinister about anyone here. Oh, they are all anxious to get their hands on extra money—to bring them back to a style of living that each one was accustomed to living. No, it must be something else that is disturbing her."

"She requested—with the use of her finger that is—that I tell no one that something is bothering her. We were supposed to discuss it, so to speak, between ourselves. She indicated that after I knew what it was and straightened it out—only then could the family get wind of it."

"There's your answer, then."

"What is the answer? Oh, Kevin, I'm so confused," she sighed, thinking then that it probably would have been a better idea if she had gone to sleep and forgotten all this until the next day."

"Whatever it is that's bothering her has something to do with you and no one else in the family. When exactly did she shed tears, Terrace? Can you recall what the conversation was about when she became upset?"

"Well . . . it seems that I was talking about my modest upbringing. Yes, that's it. I remember talking about San Francisco and the elegant homes that have a view of the bay. I told her that Aunt Agatha's house had such windows, although the house itself was nothing anyone would call elegant. Then she cried. I remember that I told her not to be upset about my life, as I did have Aunt Agatha's love—and actually my upbringing was quite pleasant."

"There it is, then. Leave it to Aunt Moira. No one would have figured the situation with her wise control."

"But I can't either, Kevin. I don't know what you're talking about."

"Yes, you can, darling. I have an idea—and if it's right, I'm sure Moira would feel completely relieved to get the burden off her shoulders after all these years. Come with me now. Put on a warm robe and come with me," he beckoned as he stood up from his chair.

"Where are we going?"

"To Moira's room," he answered casually.

"Now?"

"Good a time as any," he said and she reluctantly followed him out of the room.

Chapter 14

"Terrace, it's all catching up to you," he said softly as she leaned heavily on his arm in their walk to Moira's room. "Perhaps we should leave this until morning."

"No, I'm fine. It's just . . . it's all becoming so complicated."

"It isn't, darling. We've just figured out Moira's dilemma. After our short visit to her now, all we'll have left to do is decide when we'll marry and where."

"Those decisions don't seem too burdensome to look forward to tackling," she said, smiling up at him.

"You see, Terrace, your parents made it very easy for you, should anything ever happen to them."

"My parents? Oh, Kevin, you knew them well—and instead of learning all I could about them from you right off, my mind has been on other things."

"We'll have a lot of time together for me to relate many stories about your mother and father. They were great people. But they did travel extensively, Terrace. They were on their way to Africa when your mother left you with your Aunt Agatha. I remember your mother always being very concerned about you and the fact that they had to travel so much. Your father was into investment research for a bank. He was their troubleshooter for future investments in other countries. They always kept you in the background. Sometimes the area of your father's business could get sticky—bribery, kidnaping, and all that."

"What did you mean when you said that they made things easy for me?" she asked.

"Hush, now. We're at Moira's room. I hope I'm not going off on an illogical tangent, but I'll take that chance. We'll let Moira explain. I'm sure she'll be relieved and delighted to do so."

"But how . . . ?"

"Trust me, Terrace," was all he said as he opened the door to Moira's sitting room. The door to the bedroom area was ajar and they stood at the threshold to be met by a very wide awake and perturbed Lizbeth.

"Master Kevin, now what is it that you're up to at this time of night? And dragging this poor child with you as well as disturbing Moira—who has been, I might add, quite restless the whole night."

"Now, Lizbeth," he said, holding out his hand in front of him. "All this is nothing to get upset about."

"Indeed?" she bristled.

"As a matter of fact, our little visit with Moira will settle her restlessness, I promise you."

"Going to tell her something that will please her, are you?" she asked, her eyes going from one to the other.

"Come now, Lizbeth. Trust us. I'll come knock at your door in a short while as soon as we're through. And we'll only stay a short while."

"Humph," the girl huffed. "Middle of the night visits, falls over cliffs, broken ankles—it's getting a bit like the cinema in here," she said as she left the room.

"Moira? Moira?" Terrace was already at her aunt's side and no time passed before the woman's eyes were wide, gazing up at her niece. "Lizbeth was right. You were not fully asleep, were you, Moira?"

The woman's hands had been clasped in front of her and now Terrace saw the index finger move twice.

"Aunt Moira, I have someone with me who wants to talk to you," she said as she beckoned Kevin to move closer to the bed and within the realm of vision of the older woman. "Kevin, I think it would be a good idea if you told Moira the good news about your book," she added, placing her hand on his arm.

"Ah, Terrace. Moira and I have very few secrets from each other. She already knows about my success."

"Moira, isn't it grand about Kevin and his writing? I'm sure you're pleased."

Moira responded that she was pleased.

"We've come . . . we've come, aunt, because I've been very concerned about your short periods of unhappiness when I've been with you. I realize, Moira, that you wanted us to unravel the puzzle before anyone else in the family was told. Yet . . . for the life of me, Moira, I couldn't figure it out. I thought . . . well . . . since something very special happened to Kevin and me tonight . . . I thought it would be all right if I discussed everything with him."

"What my precious Terrace is too shy to say, Moira, is that we're in love and want to be married. But I know that Terrace would not relax knowing that there's something making you unhappy that she can't remedy."

"You don't mind, do you, Moira, that Kevin is going to help us?"

No, no, no.

"Oh, I'm so relieved, Moira. I didn't want you upset any more than necessary."

"Moira," Kevin said as he pulled up two chairs for himself and Terrace, "this problem that is upsetting you concerns Terrace, doesn't it? Ah, I thought so. By the way, I am so delighted to see that you can communicate. Do you realize, Moira, that with additional therapy you may even be able to use additional muscles?"

"Look, Kevin, her eyes are shining very brightly."

"Yes. She's pleased at her capability to communicate. Don't worry, Moira. We'll straighten out this other problem and your mind will be at ease to think only about recovering more fully."

Yes.

"I'm happy you agree, Moira. Now, it seems to me from Terrace's explanation that you seemed to sadden every time you heard her mention anything about her modest upbringing. Is that right? I thought so."

"What is it, Kevin?" Terrace cried.

"It must be only one thing," he said, his face practically contorted in thought. "Moira, Greg Connors left something with you that belongs to Terrace, is that right?"

Yes, yes.

"But, Kevin, Moira had all those years when she could have contacted me—before her stroke."

"But did she really, Terrace? Suppose something was given to her for safekeeping until you became a certain age? How old are you now, Terrace?"

"Twenty-one. Just twenty-one before I made this trip."

"There you see. Moira, were you to wait until her twenty-first birthday? Ah, I thought so."

"I still don't know why the family didn't contact me all these years, Kevin. Unless . . . my mother wasn't really welcome here, was she?"

"Not really, Terrace. She was an outsider and Pegeen put a lot of demands on her. Poor Moira was caught in the middle. After your parents died, she was going to contact Aunt Agatha to ask if you could stay here at the house in Dublin. I know for a fact that Pegeen fought against having you here."

"I assumed the problem was something of that nature," she answered quietly.

"But you have to admit, Moira was astute in letting things go the way she did."

"What do you mean?" she asked, becoming even more confused.

"Moira had something for your safekeeping until you were twenty-one. If she forced the issue with Pegeen, you were too young to defend yourself and Pegeen—if she ever found out everything—could have exploited you."

"Kevin . . ."

"I know, I'm confusing you further. Moira, let's straighten this out for Terrace. Where is it, Moira? Is it in this room?"

Yes.

"In a drawer, perhaps? No? In a secret place, hidden? Yes, no? Well, it's not in sight, but it's not in a secret hiding place."

Yes.

"Then, could it be in a book? Yes? Now we're getting somewhere."

"Kevin . . . ?"

"Not now, darling. Moira and I are too busy clearing up your life. Moira, Greg Connors was interested in Irish lore. Could it be in a book of that sort?

No.

"Of course, we could go through every book in this room. No, just one more try. If it's not in a book on Irish lore, then it's in a book that concerns your mother, Terrace. Is it in a book on the States—a history of the States?"

Yes, yes, yes.

"Where, Moira? On this side of the bookcase? No? This side, then. Yes? All right—not this shelf, nor this—yes, here, at the top in a corner." He pulled a large gray volume out of the bookcase and in no time he had opened the book and held his hand high over his head clutching a yellowed envelope.

"Kevin, is it really from my parents? Please read it to me."

But the next voice she heard was not Kevin's, but a very low sleepy muffle of Padrig Corot.

"Yes, Kevin. I guess it would be a good idea to read it and let us all know what it says."

"Padrig! What made you come here?" Kevin snarled.

"What a question to ask! There've been footsteps and mumblings and doors slamming in this house for the last few hours. So I've come to see for myself what the carryings-on are all about, being a member in good standing of this family," he added meekly.

"Padrig," Terrace said snidely.

"Now, cousin, I told you originally not to think too harshly of me. Things have been very tough for me."

181

"Yes, I'll say," retorted Kevin. "It is very tough to live in the style you prefer without lifting a finger to work for the funds to pay for all of it."

"But you don't lack for funds, do you, Kevin? One of my friends just over from the States claims you've a best seller over there. Secretive about it, weren't you?"

"No, just being practical so that you wouldn't start bleeding me like you've done Moira. I didn't know if Moira was going to need any operations—or how much medical care it would take to rehabilitate her. Anyway, Padrig, there's one more thing, something you probably wouldn't understand. I like to write—the publicity that goes with it is only secondary."

The men just looked at each other and then Padrig broke the silence. "I never did like you, Kevin. I really never did, you know."

With that, Kevin gave a loud guffaw. "The feeling was always mutual, Padrig," he answered.

"Well, now that that's over, why don't you get on with reading the letter? Don't let me stop you. I'm family, you know."

"Go ahead, Kevin. You might as well read it," Terrace sighed.

Kevin pulled out an equally yellowed letter from the envelope and glanced slowly down the page.

"Well, what is it? Tell us," Padrig stammered, the perspiration pouring down his forehead.

"It seems that this entire estate belonged to one Gregory Connors. At his death and the death of his wife, his sister Moira was to have control of everything until the twenty-first birthday of his daughter, mentioned here as Terrace Connors. At this age, Terrace Connors becomes sole beneficiary of this house, the furnishings, and all currency—a very sizable sum at the First Bank of Dublin," finished Kevin in a quiet tone.

"Well, what do you think of that, what do you think of that," Padrig kept repeating while looking straight ahead of him.

"Evidently Greg Connors wanted to protect Terrace from anyone knowing of her assets until she was old enough to take care of herself. This letter is handwritten, but the signature is notarized. Poor Moira, what frustration she must have felt when after keeping the secret all these years she was unable to tell Terrace because of her inability to speak," said Kevin.

"But she did tell me, Kevin. She spoke to me even if it was with her index finger instead of her voice. Oh, Moira, how can I thank you for . . . well, for taking care of everything for me, and—well, just for everything," she said as she leaned over and hugged the woman and kissed her lightly on her forehead. "Now it's my turn to shed tears, isn't it, Moira?"

Yes. No.

Terrace laughed at Moira's double answer. "Now, Padrig," she said as she stood once more and faced her cousin, "are you heavily in debt, Padrig?"

"Not so heavily in debt as much as heavily in want of starting something on my own to build from," he said.

"Never mind the act, Padrig," Kevin snorted. "You've already drained Terrace out of a lot of currency by sponging off Moira all these years."

"No, Kevin," Terrace interrupted. "I can't just leave him this way. He is family. And, besides, Padrig, it seems as though I've found my pot of gold, and since you were the one who first told me about the lucky fairy tree, I want you to have your pot of gold too."

"Aw, cousin, I really can't ask you to . . ."

"Hush, now. I'll only do this once, Padrig. So, if you muff this, it's your future. I want to back your pub and then with your first profits, you'll be able to pay off your own debts. Kevin, you said we are to be married. Perhaps you won't agree, but . . ."

"Nonsense," he smiled. "I have enough money from my first book to take care of you for the rest of your life. Also, my second book is almost finished and my editor is begging for the last chapters right now. So our future is taken care of very well by all that. It's your business if you want to give this good-for-nothing a legitimate start in the business world," he pouted and then his face broke out into a grin. "Okay, Padrig," he said, extending his hand, "luck be with you."

"You know, Kevin," Padrig said, reaching Kevin with his own hand, "Maybe you're not a bad chap after all."

"Never you mind," Kevin said, slapping him on the back, "I'm nasty from the core, don't you forget that."

Terrace stretched her hand out in Padrig's direction and he walked slowly over to hold it. "Padrig, this is your home," she said, "and you are my family. We all have our own weaknesses. It's time you made a fresh start."

"I'm going to make a real stab at it, cousin."

"Well, it's all settled. Will we be living here, Kevin, I mean in Dublin?"

"I don't know if it will upset you, Terrace, but I'll have to spend a great deal of time in the States. Of course, we'll be coming to Dublin quite often."

"Upset me? It's merely having the best of both worlds. But if that is the case, then I would like to provide enough to keep this house going, Moira in therapy, and Pegeen adequately covered. Also, Lizbeth must be given a large raise in salary."

"I think you're managing your assets properly," smiled Kevin. "We'll go to the solicitor's office tomorrow. Now, can we finally get down to more serious matters?" he said, winking at Padrig.

"And what is that?" she asked.

"Just a very serious thing like loving me," he said, and neither one seemed to care that Padrig was watching as she flung herself into his arms.

"I can't wait for you to meet Aunt Ag," she said.

And she couldn't wait, so that as the days passed and she and Kevin prepared to make the trip to San Francisco where they planned to marry, she felt the excitement mount steadily with each passing moment. And yet, she could not believe that soon she would be leaving this land of greenery with its misty Atlantic coast to be once again looking over San Francisco Bay and the Pacific. She could not believe it, that is, until she and Kevin were alighting at San Francisco International Airport on a beautiful clear and sunny June day.

"Do you think Aunt Agatha will like me?" he asked as they settled themselves in the taxi he had hailed after they retrieved their bags.

"If she doesn't, she'll have me to contend with, I believe," she answered as they both laughed.

"Are you happy, Terrace?" he questioned and he took her hand and held it very tightly.

"There just couldn't be any more happiness in the

world, Kevin. I feel like I've found Padrig's pot of gold, except in contentment rather than coin."

"Yes, poor Padrig. He certainly had some bad times. Yet, I think with your generosity, he made out better than I thought he would. Working won't do him any harm, Terrace. He'll acquire a sense of responsibility."

"Kevin, we're here. This is Aunt Agatha's," she said as the taxi pulled up in front of the wood-frame house.

The next few minutes were spent paying the driver and retrieving the baggage, which was quite ample since Kevin had insisted on buying Terrace a complete wardrobe of Irish tweeds and linen dresses before they left. When they finally rang the doorbell, they looked as though they had been on safari with the amount of baggage that surrounded them on the porch.

Still, Aunt Agatha never noticed the luggage as she opened the door. Instead, her eyes went from Terrace to Kevin and back to Terrace again in quick nervous movements until Terrace broke the silence.

"Aunt Ag," she said quietly. "I'm home, Aunt Ag. And this is Kevin Sanford. We've come home to be married. We'd like you to stand up for us."

There was a sudden look of relief on Agatha's face just before her features broke into a wide and pleasant smile. Then, it took her no time to regain her composure and begin to direct proceedings as to where to place the bags and in which room Kevin would be staying until the wedding.

When they all had refreshed themselves and reassembled in the parlor—and it certainly was a parlor, with very little change from the turn of the century—Agatha sat in front of the two young people, clasped her hands in front of her and took a deep sigh.

186

"Aunt Ag, I hope you didn't mind that I gave you no notice of our arrival. I just didn't want you to expect us and then have our schedule change only to disappoint you."

"Nonsense, Terrace. This was a lovely surprise. I just want you both to know that for years I've been preoccupied with the problem of how to approach the people of Merrion Square to . . . well, to sort of bridge the gap between you and the members of your father's family. Your parents' accident, Terrace, was a shock to me. I just did the best I could do for you with what I had. However, I just felt, somehow, that it was time you made a trip to Dublin."

"It's all over now, Aunt Ag. Everything worked out fine."

"Yes, it did," she beamed. "In fact, in honor of the occasion, I think I'll prepare us all some tea."

"No, Aunt Agatha. You go sit on the porch and Kevin and I will get the tea ready."

"Well, if you really insist," her aunt said and bustled out to the porch.

"She's a grand lady," Kevin said as Terrace peered out at Agatha through the sheer white curtains in the parlor.

"Kevin, come here a moment. Just look at Aunt Agatha. It's amazing," she finally said.

"What's wrong? She looks very happy in that rocking chair."

"Yes, but look how she's rocking—slowly and contentedly. Kevin, there's no frenzy in her rocking, just a peaceful swaying of the chair. Do you know, it's the first time in my life that I've ever seen her rock like that."

"Do you think she's happy, Terrace?" he asked as he placed his arm around her waist.

"Yes, I think she's finally at peace and quite happy. But not as happy as I am," she said, as she lifted her face to his.

Love—the way you want it!

Candlelight Romances

		TITLE NO.	
☐ THE CAPTIVE BRIDE by Lucy Phillips Stewart .	$1.50	#232	(17768-5)
☐ FORBIDDEN YEARNINGS by Candice Arkham.	$1.25	#235	(12736-X)
☐ HOLD ME FOREVER by Melissa Blakeley	$1.25	#231	(13488-9)
☐ THE HUNGRY HEART by Arlene Hale	$1.25	#226	(13798-5)
☐ LOVE'S UNTOLD SECRET by Betty Hale Hyatt .	$1.25	#229	(14986-X)
☐ ONE LOVE FOREVER by Meredith Babeaux Brucker	$1.25	#234	(19302-8)
☐ PRECIOUS MOMENTS by Suzanne Roberts	$1.25	#236	(19621-3)
☐ THE RAVEN SISTERS by Dorothy Mack	$1.25	#221	(17255-1)
☐ THE SUBSTITUTE BRIDE by Dorothy Mack.....	$1.25	#225	(18375-8)
☐ TENDER LONGINGS by Barbara Lynn.......	$1.25	#230	(14001-3)
☐ UNEXPECTED HOLIDAY by Libby Mansfield ..	$1.50	#233	(19208-0)
☐ CAMERON'S LANDING by Anne Stuart	$1.25	#504	(10995-7)
☐ SUMMER MAGIC by F.C. Matranga	$1.25	#503	(17962-9)
☐ LEGEND OF LOVE by Louis Bergstrom.......	$1.25	#502	(15321-2)
☐ THE GOLDEN LURE by Jean Davidson	$1.25	#500	(12965-6)
☐ MOONLIGHT MIST by Laura London........	$1.50	#263	(15464-4)
☐ THE SCANDALOUS SEASON by Nina Pykare..	$1.50	#501	(18234-4)

At your local bookstore or use this handy coupon for ordering:

Dell DELL BOOKS
P.O. BOX 1000, PINEBROOK, N.J. 07058

Please send me the books I have checked above. I am enclosing $_____
(please add 75¢ per copy to cover postage and handling). Send check or money order—no cash or C.O.D.'s. Please allow up to 8 weeks for shipment.

Mr/Mrs/Miss _____

Address _____

City _____ State/Zip _____

THE PASSING BELLS

by
PHILLIP ROCK

A story you'll wish would go on forever.

Here is the vivid story of the Grevilles, a titled British family, and their servants—men and women who knew their place, upstairs and down, until England went to war and the whole fabric of British society began to unravel and change.

"Well-written, exciting. Echoes of Hemingway, Graves and *Upstairs, Downstairs*."—*Library Journal*

"Every twenty-five years or so, we are blessed with a war novel, outstanding in that it depicts not only the history of a time but also its soul."—*West Coast Review of Books*.

"Vivid and enthralling."—*The Philadelphia Inquirer*

A Dell Book $2.75   (16837-6)

At your local bookstore or use this handy coupon for ordering:

| Dell | **DELL BOOKS** THE PASSING BELLS $2.75   (16837-6)
P.O. BOX 1000, PINEBROOK, N.J. 07058 |

Please send me the above title. I am enclosing $ _____
(please add 75¢ per copy to cover postage and handling). Send check or money order—no cash or C.O.D.'s. Please allow up to 8 weeks for shipment.

Mr/Mrs/Miss _____

Address _____

City _____ State/Zip _____

Dell Bestsellers

☐ TO LOVE AGAIN by Danielle Steel $2.50 (18631-5)
☐ SECOND GENERATION by Howard Fast $2.75 (17892-4)
☐ EVERGREEN by Belva Plain $2.75 (13294-0)
☐ AMERICAN CAESAR by William Manchester . . . $3.50 (10413-0)
☐ THERE SHOULD HAVE BEEN CASTLES
   by Herman Raucher $2.75 (18500-9)
☐ THE FAR ARENA by Richard Ben Sapir $2.75 (12671-1)
☐ THE SAVIOR by Marvin Werlin and Mark Werlin . $2.75 (17748-0)
☐ SUMMER'S END by Danielle Steel $2.50 (18418-5)
☐ SHARKY'S MACHINE by William Diehl $2.50 (18292-1)
☐ DOWNRIVER by Peter Collier $2.75 (11830-1)
☐ CRY FOR THE STRANGERS by John Saul $2.50 (11869-7)
☐ BITTER EDEN by Sharon Salvato $2.75 (10771-7)
☐ WILD TIMES by Brian Garfield $2.50 (19457-1)
☐ 1407 BROADWAY by Joel Gross $2.50 (12819-6)
☐ A SPARROW FALLS by Wilbur Smith $2.75 (17707-3)
☐ FOR LOVE AND HONOR by Antonia Van-Loon . . $2.50 (12574-X)
☐ COLD IS THE SEA by Edward L. Beach $2.50 (11045-9)
☐ TROCADERO by Leslie Waller $2.50 (18613-7)
☐ THE BURNING LAND by Emma Drummond $2.50 (10274-X)
☐ HOUSE OF GOD by Samuel Shem, M.D. $2.50 (13371-8)
☐ SMALL TOWN by Sloan Wilson $2.50 (17474-0)

At your local bookstore or use this handy coupon for ordering:

Dell | **DELL BOOKS**
P.O. BOX 1000, PINEBROOK, N.J. 07058

Please send me the books I have checked above. I am enclosing $_____
(please add 75¢ per copy to cover postage and handling). Send check or money
order—no cash or C.O.D.'s. Please allow up to 8 weeks for shipment.

Mr/Mrs/Miss _____

Address _____

City _____ State/Zip _____

INTRODUCING...

The Romance Magazine For The 1980's

Each exciting issue contains a full-length romance novel — the kind of first-love story we all dream about...

PLUS

other wonderful features such as a travelogue to the world's most romantic spots, advice about your romantic problems, a quiz to find the ideal mate for you and much, much more.

ROMANTIQUE: A complete novel of romance, plus a whole world of romantic features.

ROMANTIQUE: Wherever magazines are sold. Or write Romantique Magazine, Dept. C-1, 41 East 42nd Street, New York, N.Y. 10017

INTERNATIONALLY DISTRIBUTED BY DELL DISTRIBUTING, INC.